HIT THEM WHERE IT HURTS!

The guard broke into a huge, uncomprehending grin. But the grin quickly changed to a look of panic as Hooker grabbed the man from behind over his nose and mouth and cut deep across his throat in one fluid motion.

A river of blood flowed through the gaping second mouth Hooker had opened. The guard's hands instinctively flew to the savage wound, his mouth silently trying to muscle a scream from the severed vocal cords.

He was dead in seconds.

"It's show time," Hendricks said as he walked toward the truck.

Hooker followed immediately, pausing only long enough to bend down and wipe the bloodied blade of his knife against the dead Bokalan's pant leg.

ALSO BY BARRY SADLER:

RAZOR

A mercenary adventure with commander Martin Hendricks

Titles by Barry Sadler
from The Berkley Publishing Group

RAZOR
RESCUE

The CASCA Series

RESCUE

BARRY SADLER

JOVE BOOKS, NEW YORK

RESCUE

A Jove Book / published by arrangement with
the author

PRINTING HISTORY
Jove edition / June 1991

ISBN: 0-515-10490-6

Jove Books are published by The Berkley Publishing Group,
200 Madison Avenue, New York, New York 10016.
The name "JOVE" and the "J" logo
are trademarks belonging to Jove Publications, Inc.

PRINTED IN THE UNITED STATES OF AMERICA

10 9 8 7 6 5 4 3 2 1

DEDICATED

to

Henry Schlesinger, my friend and editor who gave this novel life while I was fighting for mine. And,

to

Duke, Robbie, Lavona, Thor, Baron, Brookie, Bob Edwards, Bob Brown, Dr. Nevis, Nurses Sandy and Sandy, the pilots of Lear Jet 31 & 32, Gene Lewis, Mr. Cone & Walsh of Professional Ambulance Service, Dr. Digenis, Dr. Weiss, Dr. Blumenkopf, the Staff at V.A. Hospital/Nashville including Angelo Grandelli, Rick, Patty, Harold, Valliere, Sadie, Coggins, Larry, Danny and all of those friends that called, wrote and came by. . . . THANKS.

Barry Sadler

PROLOGUE

The screaming stopped shortly after midnight.

Hendricks wondered who it was this time. A door opened and closed. The sound of a body being dragged came through the thick wood and metal doors of his cell. He didn't have to see to know what was happening. They were taking the man Okediji had trimmed back to his cell or to a truck at the rear of the prison, where his body would be hauled off to be thrown to the animals or dumped in a nameless grave.

Huddled in the corner, Anthony tried to keep his terror under control, having done anything he could with his hands to block out the sounds of the screaming, which had started three hours before. The mottled side of his face crusted with dried blood. He had not been given the experience of one of the Barber's close shaves, not yet, anyway.

When they'd brought Hendricks back to his cell, he'd kept his control. He used part of their water to wash away the crusted blood from the artistic slices Okediji had made in his flesh. With Hendricks, Okediji had been somewhat more gentle than usual. He would need the mercenary leader as his star subject when they went on trial. He had left the face alone, as he had on all those he planned on saving.

1

As for the rest, they were of no more value, other than the small pleasures they provided his men. It was good for the men to see that they were the masters and the whites were the slaves, to do with as they wished. Okediji felt it was very important for the men in his command to know they were the better, the stronger of the races. There could well come a time when they would go into battle against other whites.

The shuffling faded, followed by more determined steps. The click of hard-soled shoes on the concrete hallway came closer. There was hesitation, and Hendricks straightened up. They were stopping outside of his cell door.

The hatch used to slide in food and water opened. From the glow of the fifty-watt bulb in the hallway, Hendricks could see it was Okediji.

"My dear friends. How are we this evening? I do hope you are enjoying your visit to Bokala and will be with us a long, long time." Okediji laughed in boyish delight at his humor. "However, I am sorry to say it appears that we have lost one of our guests. He has decided to move on to a quieter existence, which I am sure you will appreciate. He was, after all, a very noisy customer, and I am certain that he has kept our other guests awake this night."

Hendricks said nothing, only locked his eyes on those of Okediji, sending out waves of hate. It was all he had to fight with.

The hatch closed, Okediji's laughter mocking as it faded down the hallway. When the thin beam of light the hatch had let in cut off again, the darkness became incredibly heavy, suffocating. The wooden slats of Hendricks's cot pressed into his thighs and felt good. Okediji had missed one thing. Sometimes pain can be used as a weapon to keep the mind sharp and to prevent it from falling into the deep recesses of apathy. Hendricks relived every one of the cuts Okediji had made in his flesh. He savored the smile of the Barber's lips as the cold German steel was turned and twisted to extract the maximum amount of pain.

"What do you think they are going to do with us now?" Anthony asked quietly.

There was just enough light seeping through the bottom and top seams of the cell door for Hendricks to make out Anthony in his prison clothes— shapeless charcoal gray pajama bottom and top. Anthony's body was huddled on his bunk, knees drawn up under his chin, arms around them, holding.

"I don't know. From what you told me, there may be a chance for you to get out. But you had better decide soon whether or not you're going to tell Okediji about your father. One thing I've learned over the years is that money can open many doors. Perhaps it will open this one for you."

He heard the boy shuffle nervously. "But what about the rest of you? I know that I can get my father to come up with one or two million. Do you think Okediji would let the rest of you go for that?"

Leaning back against the cool stones of the wall, Hendricks shook his head in the darkness.

"No way. He's going to have his show and that is one thing that can't be bought. We're the co-stars in his life story. You, he might sell. Us, never!"

There was silence save for the sounds of the men in uneasy sleep, trying to control cries of pain when

they moved. Hendricks knew Duke and Becaude
were two cells down from him. Who was in the next
cell, he didn't know. He had tried to talk to him, but
there had been no response, only whimpering and
strange gurgling noises. They found out why the
next day. One of the guards with a bit of English
and much sign language delighted in re-enacting
the event for him and Anthony. The man in the next
cell had cursed Okediji during their interrogation.
For that, his tongue had been cut out with the
Barber's razor. As for his cell-mate, his body had
been sliced into a thousand thin shreds by the razor.
It had taken eleven hours, Okediji was a patient
man.

Sleep came unwillingly. Around him Hendricks
saw the Simbas of that dawn in the Congo. He was
standing in the ring of his dead, blade in hand,
waiting for his moment to join them. He had failed
them. He failed now. It was hard, a torture worse
than anything Okediji had done to him. To prepare
for death not once, but twice, then to have it
snatched away by chance.

His eyes jerked open. The sound came again.
Thhhhp! Almost inaudible, but he knew what it
was. Sliding across the floor, he put his hand over
Anthony's mouth to stop any outcry. "Wake up," he
hissed. "Something's going down."

The food hatch opened, letting in the dim light. A
head was outlined in it. "Boss! You there!"

Washington tried to see through the gloom of the
cell's interior.

"Yes, we're here!"

Then the door opened. Washington stood there
smiling, showing his great white teeth.

Another figure was behind him, a long-nosed pistol in its hand. Kelo looked at Hendricks quickly. Then he whispered, "We must go now. There is no time."

Followed by Anthony, Hendricks stumbled into the the hall. "What about the others?"

Kelo shook his head. "Just you and the boy. We can take no others."

Hendricks started to protest, but Kelo turned on him. "There is no other way. I have arranged for you to be taken out. There is no room for the rest, and if I open their cells, there is nowhere for them to go or hide their white faces in this land. Come with me and you may be able to do something to save them. Stay and you will die. It is up to you. I do not care. I have lived up to a promise I made to myself. Now, come or stay. I am leaving."

Two cells down, a voice came to him from behind the bolted food hatch. "Go with him, Boss. We want you to. Then come back and get us or kill that son of a bitch for us." Duke moved aside to let Becaude near the hatch.

"Oui, Chef! Go with them. We will wait. It will take them time for Okediji to stage his spectacle. We will live till you come back. Now, for us, go!"

Washington took Hendricks's arm, leading up the stairs past the two bodies of the rebels he and Kelo had killed with their silenced pistols. For the first time, Hendricks saw that Washington was wearing the same camouflaged uniform as Kelo. They went up another flight to the check-in room. Three men lay dead, small black holes draining in their foreheads. In a corner, another rebel lay on his side, hands and feet tied, mouth gagged. Hendricks didn't have time to ask why this man had been permitted to live.

Quickly, he and Anthony were hustled out into the dark and shoved in the back of a waiting weapons carrier. Kelo took the wheel. Washington rode shotgun, his pistol held in his lap.

In the back, Hendricks and Anthony could see nothing. The flap had been pulled down. It was all up to the men in front, but Hendricks wondered about Kelo. He had seen him with Okediji. Who was he? Why was he doing this? Whose side was he on, if he had a side? The questions were too much, and the pain in his body drained him of the will to think clearly. All that would have to be answered later.

Twice they were stopped at checkpoints. At one, they were let through. At the other, Hendricks heard the small whisper of a silenced pistol working, then the grinding of gears as they drove on. It was an hour before dawn when they pulled off the road, passing huts and bomas surrounded by thorn brush. How long it had taken them to reach there he didn't know. His mind had drifted in and out during the ride. Anthony had caught him once when he almost fell off the bench onto the metal floor of the weapons carrier.

The back flap was opened as soon as they came to a stop.

"We're here, Boss. Let's go." Strong, gentle black hands helped him from the rear of the truck onto the ground. Washington put Hendricks's right arm over his shoulder and half carried him across the field. They were followed by Anthony, the rear being brought up by Kelo, who had exchanged his pistol for an assault rifle. They watched the roads in the distance for any rising dust trails, which would show they were being pursued.

Another hand came to help, taking some of the weight off Washington.

"All right. Let's get him inside the back seat. Young man, you take the front. Washington, there's a first aid kit and antibiotics in the back. Do what you can for him. It's time to get the hell out of here."

The voice was familiar. It brought Hendricks back from the edge of blackness. "Robbie?"

"Yeah, I'm here. Now shut up and rest. We're going home!"

Head resting against the rear window, Hendricks saw Kelo standing there alone on the dirt road Robbie had used to set down the twin-engined Cessna. Kelo raised the hand with the rifle in it, as a salute of farewell. Hendricks remembered when, such a short time ago, he himself had done the same to Robinson as he'd taken off without the hostages, leaving them behind.

He still couldn't put his finger on the who, what, or why of Kelo. It was too much. His eyes closed before the wheels left the ground, and the small aircraft was on its way out of Bokala.

When his eyes opened, they were over desert country. The sun was midway to noon. His head was clear for the first time since they'd been taken prisoner. Seeing him awake, Washington handed him a thermos full of hot coffee. Gratefully he put the scalding liquid to his mouth. It burned his lips but felt good. Robbie looked back over his shoulder.

"Looks like you're going to be all right. We'll be touching down in a couple of hours."

Ignoring the pain in his chest and back, he straightened up, wiping his face with his hands to clear it of the last of the fog.

"Will someone tell me what is going on? And I want to know about Kelo and you, Washington."

Washington laughed deeply.

"Hell, Boss. All that happened was that I changed into a dead rebel's uniform just before they overran us. I hid behind some trash, and they passed me by. Then I just got up and ran with them, yelling for white blood with the rest of them. As soon as I got my chance, I cut out and ran straight into Kelo, who recognized me. He grabbed me by the arm, told me to follow him and keep quiet. I did.

"Later, when we left the field, we talked over the situation. Then he managed to raise the colonel here on his radio. Between them they set up the escape. Kelo figures somehow he owes you something. He don't really care what happens to the rest. He's just paying back a debt he feels is due you personally. We only took the young white boy because he was in the same cell with you. That's it, clean and simple."

"What about the man you left tied up?"

"Shee-it! I was the only face he saw, so we left him alive to keep Kelo in the clear about who snatched you. I even left a message to him in English on the desk, saying I was one of your men who escaped the field and came back for my leader. That way they won't be looking too close at Kelo."

Leaning forward, Hendricks touched Robinson on the shoulder. "What about you? Won't you get in trouble with your superiors for this?"

Not looking back, Robinson adjusted the trim a

bit. "I would if I had any. But after hearing from Kelo, I sent in my resignation after having a talk with the Pentegon. If I get you out with no trouble, they tear up my resignation. If I get caught, then I am just another ex-serviceman who got himself into shit, and they don't know anything about it. By the way, I have a message for you from Kelo. He says he'll be waiting for you."

Hendricks touched the scars and cuts on his chest with a forefinger, running it over the ridges where Okediji's razor had sliced into him. He hadn't died, and this time he would go back to either get his men out and kill Okediji or die with them. There was no other way for him.

Anthony looked at him from the front seat. His eyes had grown very old in the last few days. He had lost his youth in Bokala. He saw the expression on Hendricks's face. His own grew harder. "I'm going with you. I lost a lot back there, too. Maybe if I go back, I can find part of it."

Grasping the shoulder of the boy-turned-man the way he had Calvin's, he nodded his head. He understood.

A black hand went on top of his. A pact had been made. They had all lost something in Bokala, and there was only one way to get it back.

Hendricks heard Robinson whisper from the pilot's seat, "Piss on General Forbes and the horse he rode in on. The bastards are going to accept my resignation!"

Then, all heard him whisper, under his breath, "Vive la mort, vive la guerre, vive le mercenaire. . . ."

ONE

NOVEMBER

Beneath them the landscape was covered by the night. A darkness spread out to the edge of the world. Under and over their wings dry winds whispered and fled.

Eight thousand feet below them people were being born and, in this drought-stricken region of Africa, even more were dying. In the *kraals* and villages there were those who dreamed, and tens of thousands more whose dreams had died.

Martin Hendricks wished at the moment that he had lost the ability to dream. For he knew that until something was done he would have nightmares. Robinson had told him that only five of his wounded had made it out with the hostages on the surviving C-130. The rest were in the prison of Bokala. How many he didn't know. But if something was not done soon, there would be none left alive.

Robbie was looking straight at the windshield of the plane. There wasn't much for him to do. A minor correction here, an adjustment of the altitude there. Come on to the VOR signal and wait. It was a long way back to Bir Misaha, the Air Force base in the southern deserts of Egypt.

Anthony Collier III had his mouth slightly open, snoring softly. Washington's head was leaning on the

11

Plexiglas side window, the blackness of his face making him almost invisible. If it hadn't been for the minute glow of the instrument panel lights, he would have been invisible.

Three of them coming out. He hadn't expected Robinson to come back for them. This time he figured they had bought it. When you live on the edge, you're never very far from falling off.

But Robinson had come back for them. The regular Air Force lieutenant colonel had told the brass at the Pentagon to stuff it. Of course the brass had no choice but to accept that. If they hadn't, Robbie had threatened to blow the whole operation and expose the American government's participation in the raid on Bokala.

Hendricks questioned himself as before, about why Robinson had been contacted on the radio by Jalingo Kelo, using the same frequency as before the raid. Any why Kelo felt he owed a debt to Hendricks and wanted to pay it off. As for the others, they apparently did not concern Kelo. But as Hendricks said to Robinson, one was better than nothing. Kelo had been as good as his word.

Robinson had come in with the Cessna Twin, landing on the outskirts of Bokala. There he had been met by Kelo and Washington. Both in the uniform of the Leopard Commandos of Okediji, Kelo with rank badges showing his new grade of major. Washington had to be content with the stripes of corporal. From there they had driven to the prison. Kelo, using his new authority, had gotten them into the lower cells, where the mercs were penned up. As Kelo had said, all of them couldn't go. Only Hendricks and the boy who'd been in the same cell with him.

Washington had escaped capture at the airfield and remained on the outside, waiting for a chance to do something. He'd been able to get away with it by changing into a dead Simba's uniform and being able to speak the language. He and Kelo had come and taken Hendricks and Anthony Collier III out of the cell.

It was two hours after dawn when they touched down for fuel at the small strip where they had refueled when Hendricks and Robinson had come in for their initial meeting with Kelo.

Kelo had instantly become a man of influence in the new regime, for it was he who had killed the premier, Afiam Mehendi, removing him from his vale of tears and eliminating any organized resistance by the Shanga tribe.

Robbie's friend the giant Sudanese captain was still there. Smiling as always, KeiKei stood with his hand close to his weapon as if he expected someone hostile to come out of the bush any second and insult him. This time he made no jokes. When he saw their faces, he knew that the men had been through a bad time, and he was certain he knew what.

For the last few days, the airwaves had been full of the rescue of the hostages from Bokala. The news had also told of the capture of the mercenaries, who were at that time being held in prison, awaiting their trial for acts of terrorism.

KeiKei knew more than a little about the recent history of Bokala and those who ran the country past and present. Just giving Robbie an understanding look, he ordered the small plane refueled and turned away, so that he could in the future deny that he had known anything about the men in the aircraft, who they were, or where they were going.

They were just four men who paid for the servicing of the plain in U.S. dollars and left. Three whites and one black. Prospectors, hunters, tourists. Whatever, he would not know if asked.

All got out of the cramped quarters of the plane to stretch their legs. Robbie took Hendricks around to the rear of the building, which served as both the control center and barracks for the troops maintaining the small field. There he gave Hendricks a bundle of clothes and pointed to a tin basin on a wooden stand with several five-gallon cans of water next to it.

"Here, I took these out of your quarters. You'll probably feel better after you clean up a little. I didn't bring anything for the boy because I didn't think he would be coming with us. I'll try to plan better next time."

He left Hendricks alone to clean up and returned to his plane and KeiKei. After a few words, the Sudanese went into his quarters and came back with a set of drab olive mechanic's coveralls that would probably fit the young man. They weren't much, but they were clean. Thanking KeiKei, Robbie turned them over to Anthony and pointed him around to the rear of the building, where Hendricks was washing up.

Hendricks was surprised at the change in his appearance. His face had grown thinner in the short time he had been the guest of Okediji. The slices in his chest, where Okediji had peeled away a few inches of surface skin from the redder flesh beneath, burned. Okediji, Hendricks was convinced, would have to die, not only for what had been done to him but for what he was going to do to Duke and Becaude and the others.

He would certainly make them suffer for Hendricks's escape. But there had been no other way. He'd had to leave without them. That was the only chance they would have. If he could get out, he might be able to put together another team quickly and go back for them. Before that happened some of them were going to die. Of that he had no doubt. But there was a good chance that Okediji would keep most of them alive for the trial he wished to stage. It was hard to wish death for anyone you knew, but he hoped that if—no! When death did come to the cells beneath the floors of the prison, it would pass by Duke and Becaude until he returned. And he had no doubt that he would come back. There were too many scores yet to settle to let the matter rest. Scores must always be settled, especially those where the currency was blood.

Robbie was right. Changing out of the prison clothes into his own khakis and boots did give him a surge of strength and energy. It was odd how small things could affect one's attitude so greatly.

After squaring accounts with KeiKei, they climbed back into the Cessna. This time Hendricks took the right seat, beside Robinson, and had Anthony sit in the rear with Washington. It was time to start asserting himself again—to take command of the situation rather than just take what chance dealt him.

By the time they were in the pattern for the air

base at Bir Misaha, the African sun was midday-high over the crest of the world. It filled the sky as it does not do in any other place in the world. The sun dominated everything and everyone. Hendricks could understand how the ancients had believed it to be a god. It gave life and death equally. And this land had seen more than its share of death. The secrets the sands of the Sahara covered would never be fully revealed. Hendricks believed that if all the blood spilled out onto the sands ever came to the surface, there would be indeed a new Red Sea.

As soon as they touched down, a weapons carrier and jeep were there to intercept them. A squad of sharp-looking blue-bereted Air Commandos met them with arms at the ready. They were under the command of a major wearing cammies, his beret set at a cocky angle, the flap of his pistol holster open as though he expected a Western style shoot out.

The major was officious and eager. His face had that recently boiled look of one new to the desert. Thin whisps of close-cropped, washed-out, bland blond hair stuck out under the leather rim of his beret.

"You are all under arrest and will come with me. If you have any weapons, you will at this time surrender them to me."

Hendricks looked at Robinson. "What the bloody hell is this? I thought you had cleared this shit with General Forbes."

Robinson shrugged eloquently. "I thought I had, but with brass, who knows? Anyway, I think we can still get what we want. For now, let's not give the prick any excuse to play Audie Murphy. You need to get those cuts looked at, and we all need some sleep before we can think clearly."

He gave the major a withering stare before stating with disgust to Hendricks, "You know it turns my gut when I think I was a lot like this asshole just a few days ago. Don't worry about it. I promise you I'll have this squared away fast."

They loaded into the weapons carrier under the stern, sweaty eye of the Commandos and were driven over the sticky tarmac to the makeshift terminal, which served as HQ, mess hall and dispensary. At Robinson's insistence, Hendricks was taken to the dispensary to have his wounds treated. Meanwhile, Robinson was taken to what had been, until two days ago, his office, to meet with the new base commander.

TWO

Major Parrish, following his orders, kept Hendricks and Robinson separated. The boy and Washington he put in together. Parrish had a small supply room cleared out and a couple of bunks brought over from the barracks area. He could have kept them at the barracks, but it was too open. Here he could keep them under control with a minimal guard.

Major Parrish had nothing personal against his detainees. Actually he envied them a bit. All professional military men have at one time or another dreamed about going on a desperate mission. These men had done that very thing. He would have liked to talk to them—to find out what it was like to make a raid, to fight a desperate battle on an airfield in central Africa, to be captured, then to escape the hands of a madman. He would have liked to, but he wouldn't. He was, even if he had not been fortunate enough to have seen combat, a career officer. He would follow his orders, which at this time were to put Robinson in communication with General Forbes in Washington at 1600 hours GMT.

As for the rest, he had no idea of what was to be done with them. He would have to wait for further instructions.

• • •

Down the maze of corridors—where it was seriously whispered in hushed voices that the souls of lost administrative officers still wandered after thirty years of trying to find their offices—General Forbes's piercing cry of "Jesus Christ!" made several of the more religious office workers touch silver stars of David hanging from thin chains about their necks or furtively cross themselves in that peculiar human trait of trying to ward off evil or bad luck.

General Forbes was trying to keep his blood pressure from rising to the point of a stroke. His S-2, Lieutenant Colonel Simpson—a ring knocker from the class of '67—stood by, thinking of the fate of bearers of bad news in the past. He was just delivering it. He did not originate it.

"That damn Robinson did it. He actually got Hendricks out of Bokala. I didn't think he had it in him. It would have been better if he'd just simply got his ass blown away. But no, he went in and he came out. Not only did he bring Hendricks—that we could probably control—but he has two others with him, and one of them is the son of Anthony Collier II. Jesus Christ!" he bellowed again. "That tears it. Why wasn't I informed that Old Man Collier's son was in the area?"

The S-2 shrugged eloquently. "Well, General, you were not informed because I was not informed. The Collier boy is a civilian and was not, as I have since discovered, even supposed to be in Bokala. He and his girl friend were doing the cross-Africa thing, and Bokala was not on the itinerary he gave his father. There was simply no way for us to know of his presence there."

Satisfied that he had done some homework prior to presenting the decoded message from Bir Misaha, the S-2 gave himself a mental pat on the back. It was always good to be better informed than your superiors.

He knew the background of Collier quite well, and the general was right. There was indeed going to be a very severe problem and possibly some early retirements if they did not handle this one very carefully. The elder Collier was simply too rich, too powerful and too a good a friend with too many congressmen, governors and even presidents, past and present.

Once this information was passed on to another man, whose parents also had very little imagination concerning names, Mr. Phillip R. Anderson II, everyone's balls would be in a vise.

Anderson was the "man" in charge of the program that had sent Hendricks and his mercenaries into Bokala to rescue the hostages Mehendi had been holding. And, as with most men in a position of confidence and trust at State, he had delegated most of the responsibility to General Forbes, whose ass would take it on the line if anything went wrong.

Forbes held his head between his hands. Fingers working into his scalp, as if by the pressure of his fingers he could pull a solution out of the flesh and bone.

"It would have been so much easier if it had just been Hendricks and the other mercenary, Washington. We could have arranged for them to quietly disappear. The desert is big and empty, you know?"

This he said with a touch of hope in his voice, then sighed deeply. "No way now. But maybe, just maybe we can get the old man's kid to keep quiet about what happened. If he does, we may still be able to salvage the operation."

Lieutenant Colonel Simpson knew he meant not salvage, but keep quiet.

"If I may make a suggestion, sir?" He left it hanging.

Forbes, with a flash of hope in his eyes, looked from his desk to the thin-faced Simpson. "Yes by all means, Colonel. I am open to anything reasonable."

"Well, sir, this came down to you from Anderson at State. It would appear to me that you have lived up to your responsibilities, with the small exception of Colonel Robinson's unorthodox behavior. But that does not have to be mentioned. We do after all have his resignation in hand. As for Mr. Anderson, we inform him only that Hendricks made it out of Bokala and, in the process, brought the boy with him. Now, what does he want done with them? Push the ball back into State's court. From that point on, the decisions and responsibility will be theirs."

Forbes gleamed, his back straightened. Of course! he thought. It's so simple. Give the problem back, and just to make sure it would not return to him, he would quietly put in his own papers for retirement. He didn't need this aggravation.

"Good thinking, Simpson!" He addressed the S-2 by his last name, something he seldom did and then only when Simpson had pulled his ass out of another problem. "That'll work. Get your report together and run over to Anderson's office and brief him. I'll wait here in case anything else comes down while you're gone."

Giving a class salute, Simpson about-faced out of Forbes's office, thinking, Sure you'll wait and let me do the dirty work. But if I have any luck at all and if I know you, you will be hanging it up very soon, and that means new slots open up. Maybe I can make full bird before my time is up.

When Simpson left Anderson's offices, it was with a distinct feeling of relief. Anderson at first began to boil. He had a feather in his cap now for the successful rescue of the hostages. The few mercenaries who had made it out with them had each been debriefed and threatened in no uncertain terms about what would happen to them if they broke Hendricks's agreement to remain silent. Of course, none of them knew about Anderson. All they knew was that they had been on what they thought, but couldn't prove, was an American air base somewhere in the southern Sahara. As to who had sanctioned or was paying for the operation, they had no idea. According to the reports he'd received, they didn't really care. They had made it out by the proverbial foreskin and were happy to be alive and free.

The reports from Bokala were an entirely different matter. After the coup against Mehendi, the new president, Mr. Leopoldo Okediji had screamed to high heavens over the interference in his country by foreign mercenaries. Stating that he would have taken care of the hostage problem, he promised that whoever had sponsored the operation would have to pay and pay dearly for interfering in the rights of an independent African state.

No one, of course, at that point had been paying too much attention to Okediji. There were a few holes in his statements. At the time of the rescue, he was not president. As to his taking care of the hostage crisis, there were few in the Western world who would put much faith in that. His reputation as a rabid racist was well known, and there had been several reports about Europeans who had fallen into the hands of his rebels. None of them were ever seen again. Horrible stories about their fate continued to circulate, but there was no substantiation for them. Therefore, there was little that anyone outside of Bokala could do about it.

The escape of Hendricks had brought Anderson a few problems, but even that might be used to his advantage. Now that their leader was out, he could control the mouths of his men and make certain they remained silent. As for the son of Anthony Collier II, that situation could certainly be made to work to his benefit. He would arrange a meeting immediately and be the bearer of glad tidings to the anxious father.

Over the last weeks, Collier had made numerous strong requests that his son be located. Well, now he had him. And if he played it right, he could make Collier aware, without saying it, that he was the one responsible for the rescue. A man who had controlling interest in a large number of radio and television stations, as well as newspapers and film companies, would certainly be an asset. Especially if one had larger political ambitions.

Yes, indeed. This might turn out to be quite fortuitous, an opportunity to build a relationship with the power men of the commercial world. He had no doubt that many of those who now sat in the hallowed halls of political power had been aided in getting there, if not directly put there, by the influence and donations of Anthony Collier II and his many friends of like wealth and interests.

It took a few minutes for his secretary to find the number for Collier Enterprises's office in New York. As soon as the call was placed, Anderson took over the line to speak to Collier's personal secretary. The voice on the other end was masculine, educated and confident. Collier's male secretary talked more like a diplomat than most of the senators Anderson knew. This secretary probably had more power.

"Mr. Jameson, this is Phillip Anderson from the State Department. I wish to speak with Mr. Collier. It is in reference to his son. We have some information."

There was a pause before the cultivated voice said, "Of course, Mr. Anderson. If you will wait a moment, I will connect you."

Soft music came over the line to fill the void. Anderson knew that, in just a moment's time, he might be well on his way to achieving goals that had been far outside his limited reach just minutes before.

The voice, which came on the line in less than five seconds, was strong. The voice of a man who got what he wanted. There was a tremor to it, as the man tried to control his emotions. He was expecting the worst. *Good*, thought Anderson. That will make him appreciate even more what I am going to give him.

"Mr. Anderson, Collier here. Jameson said you have information pertaining to my son. What is it?"

Anderson gloated. The man could not control his impatience. "Yes, of course, Mr. Collier. Let me say first your son is well and in the protection of Americans. However, I do feel that we should have a meeting in person so that I might fill you in on the details."

The voice came back, stronger this time, more determined now that fear for his son's safety was diminished. "Where is he? And when can I talk to him?"

"Really, Mr. Collier, it is best if we discuss this in person. Your son has been involved in a sensitive situation, which I think will be best explained when we meet. I can be in New York in two hours. Trust me, sir. I have your and your son's best interests at heart. To move precipitously at this point would be unwise."

Anderson liked his words. Leave some fear and doubt in the old man's mind. It would make him more pliable.

Barely controlling his sense of urgency and frustration, Collier replied curtly. "Very well, Mr. Anderson. Give Jameson the details of your flight, and I will have you met. Please do not tarry."

Tarry. Anderson thought. What a quaint word. One doesn't hear it very often in today's world.

"Of course, Mr. Collier."

Jameson came back on the line. Anderson told him he would be taking the three o'clock shuttle to La Guardia.

"Very good, sir. I will meet you myself at the gate."

It was a very relieved General Forbes who received a call from Anderson thanking him for his assistance and valuable services and telling him that as of this moment, he, Phillip R. Anderson II, would take over and relieve the general of his responsibilities in the matter. Everything from this point on would be run through his office.

General Forbes thanked him and continued filling out the forms for his retirement. It looked as if things were going to work out for him after all.

Jameson was not hard to spot as Anderson came through the gate. In fact it would have been impossible not to spot him. If Anderson had not known he was a secretary, he would have thought him to be a manager of a major international corporation.

Jameson wore a beautifully tailored blue worsted suit of an English cut—probably Savile Row, thought Anderson—shoes of soft black Spanish leather and a subdued burgundy silk tie, which rested on a shirt of crystal-white Italian silk. The man was thin, with gray-flecked black hair and piercing blue eyes. Anderson figured the clothes and Julian Picard watch alone would equal four to six months of Jameson's salary.

Anderson put on his best diplomat smile, designed to thaw suspicious hearts, and saw that it instantly failed. Jameson shook hands as if it was a job he did not particularly care for, but the hand was strong. As soon as it had performed its duty, it released quickly the soft, sweaty hand of Anderson and moved to Jameson's side almost as if it wanted to wipe itself clean on the blue worsted trouser, but it did not.

Taking the lead, Jameson walked Anderson through the terminal to the curb, where a silver-gray Mercedes limousine was waiting in the no parking zone. Standing to the side, he opened the door to the rear, saying only, "Mr. Collier, Mr. Anderson."

Anderson left New York feeling more than satisfied. He had played the old man like a fiddle. He had taken Collier to Fort Hamilton; from there he had arranged a communications link through a scrambler to the air base at Bir Misaha. There had been a few anxious moments before the boy came on the line. Thoughtfully, Anderson left the room to permit them to talk privately. He would listen to the tape recording of the conversations back in his office in Washington.

After the old man had been convinced his son was well, he had actually returned to Anderson with tears in his eyes. How touching!

"Mr. Anderson, I wish to assure you that I shall not forget this. If ever in the future I may be of service to you, I would consider it a privilege."

Anderson felt light-headed for a moment before regaining control of his emotions.

"Of course, Mr. Collier. I appreciate your sentiments, but I assure you that I am no more than a public servant doing what I can. Now, if you will permit me, I will make the arrangements to bring your son home as soon as possible."

He let Collier listen in as he called General Forbes at the Pentagon.

Careful to use his best and most efficient manner as he spoke, Anderson said to Forbes, "General, I want you to get our people back to the States as soon as possible. I would like for them to come in to Andrews Air Force Base so that I may debrief them personally. Please expedite the matter. I will expect them here by tomorrow morning. Thank you, General. Have a nice day."

"There. It is done Mr. Collier. Your son will be home by tomorrow morning. I presume that you would like to be on hand when he comes in. If so, that too can be arranged."

Collier shook his head of grey, carefully cut hair up and down. "Yes, of course, Mr. Anderson. If I might offer a service, I know that you wish to return to Washington. My own plane is available to take you there."

Anderson felt his chest expand two inches. "Why, yes, Mr. Collier, that might help to expedite matters. I shall take you up on your offer. It's very gracious of you."

Within the hour, he was in a private Lear jet coming into the pattern over Dulles Field. He had, by all means, let Collier offer him the use of his private jet, feeling it was only the first of many other gestures of appreciation that the old man would show him in the future. It had been a very good day, indeed.

THREE

Okediji raged, his face gray under dark skin; his eyes rolled wildly as bits of froth gathered at the corners of his mouth. He screamed at his officers around the mahogany conference table.

"You let them escape. Get away! How dare you fail me?" His eyes moved suspiciously over the faces of the men sitting at the table. Fear was a vital animal that touched each of them. They all knew it would take only a single wrong word, a nervous look. Anything could set Okediji off, and the killing would begin.

Kelo stood slightly to his rear and to the right, a French MAT-49 smg held in his hands, angled across his chest, the bolt cocked, ready for use if Okediji gave the order. Kelo hoped he would.

"I place my confidence in you and you fail me. Must I do everything myself? Why have I taken the trouble to bring you to greatness when you are incapable of handling even the simplest of assignments? Two of my prisoners have escaped. And one of them was the leader of the mercenaries. Do you have any idea what this can mean?" He answered his own question: "Of course, you do not. You ignorant animals.

"It means that now there will be those in the

outside world who may ask questions of me that I do not wish to answer. We are now a national government. We need the aid of the outside world. Their money, weapons, markets, without them we shall never achieve the objectives that will make Bokala a great power."

Okediji paused in his oration; sweat ran down his face to stain the white collar of his pima cotton shirt.

"Another thing, and do not forget it. This Martin Hendricks is no fool. It was only by good fortune that he was taken and his men captured. He is a professional soldier, and now he has a reason to hate us." He pointed his finger around the table; Kelo's smg followed the shaking finger as Okediji lectured his officers as if they were simple native children.

"He achieved his mission. He rescued the hostages and got them out. Do not forget that. The rescue was his primary objective. He could have saved his own men, but he did not. He completed his mission, and in the doing, he, as the Americans say, kicked the shit out of Mehendi. He took the airfield and held it. He wiped out security at the airfield and the palace guards. That alone would have brought down Mehendi even if we had not been ready to move in. I have the feeling that this Hendricks will not forget us. And if possible, he will try to do us harm. We do not as yet know who was his sponsor. But we will find out. One thing more we must consider is that we have no information on the boy that escaped with him. It is unfortunate that at the time I was involved with other interrogations. However, he did not have the look of a mercenary, nor was he in any kind of a uniform.

"Be alert. Do not make any more mistakes, and remember that there may be those among us who are not completely loyal. If you have any doubts about anyone, come to me personally, and I will hear you for I am your father."

His eyes narrowed to thin slits. "And as a father, I will reward and I will punish my children as they deserve. Major Moshani, stand up!"

The officer in charge of the prison felt his legs turn to water; he feared that he would foul himself. Somewhere he found the strength to pull himself erect, square his shoulders and face his leader. The back of his tunic was stuck to his spine with cold, acrid sweat.

"Moshani, you failed me. I want your successor to understand what will happen to him if he does likewise. Major Kelo, do your duty."

Okediji turned his back and walked, without turning, to the door leading to the hallway. Moshani held his hands in front of him, pale palms up. He wanted to plead, but his mouth was too dry to form words. Only a low primal whine began to form somewhere deep inside as he waved his hands back and forth in front of him, as if this might ward off that which was coming.

Kelo made no production of it. Without hurry but not slowly, he swung the bore of the MAT-49 so the muzzle was aligned with Moshani's solar plexus. His finger took up trigger slack. A three-round burst was sufficient. Two of the fingers on Moshani's left hand were blown off microseconds before his heart was ripped to shreds inside his body cavity. Blood burst out his back, spraying the wall behind him.

Moshani fell without a word. As he had feared, he

fouled himself as death released his conscious control over his sphincter muscles. Now, it no longer
mattered to him.

Kelo was well pleased. It now appeared that, along
with his promotions, he had been placed in the
position of highest trust and responsibility, that of
Okediji's personal executioner.

He knew that Okediji was right. They had not
heard the last of Hendricks. From the little time he
had spent with the man, he knew that Hendricks
was not one to forget or forgive. And, as with
Mehendi, that could serve to his advantage. He had
destroyed Mehendi with the help of Hendricks, and
perhaps he would also be able to do the same to
Okediji.

Once that was accomplished, he would at last be
in position to take over power and secure his own
people's rightful ascendance.

Patience, patience. He had waited years for the
right time to destroy Mehendi. If necessary, he could
wait years to do the same to Okediji. However,
having met Hendricks, he thought it might not take
that long.

If Hendricks was going to do anything, he would
have to do it very quickly in order to save his men.
Kelo would have to be ready to move. The money he
had taken from Mehendi when the president tried to
escape had already been sent on to where it would do
the most good. In a matter of a few weeks, the arms
it had purchased would be arriving at the borders.

This would be the last time his people would be
treated as animals. As had happened with Mehendi,
once Okediji was dead or out of the way his power
would collapse like a house of cards. There would be

a power vacuum that, if Kelo moved fast enough, he would fill.

Even now he was gaining more influence daily with all the officers of Okediji's high command. That was a powerful designation for men who were fit only to command mindless sheep. Of Okediji's staff of ten commandants, only three could read or write. The others had to have the orders read to them by aides.

Kelo had learned one tactic long ago. When you are a people small in numbers and wealth, you must divide and conquer. Mehendi was done with, and the tribesmen of Okediji would quickly see to the reduction of their numbers so that they would never again present a threat.

Once that was done, there would only remain the elimination of Okediji. Already they had lost thousands of young men in the revolution. They would lose more before they finished the population control measures against the remnants of Mehendi's tribe.

Patience, patience. All was coming his way. Even now, the numerical superiority of the opposition was marginal. Kelo had kept his people out of the struggle. Tens of thousands were in refugee camps across the borders of Nigeria and Chad. They had been saved.

Soon, they would come back, not as refugees being repatriated to their homeland, but as warriors, and he would at last be able to end his charade.

For the second time, he'd had to play a role for the enemy despots. As an officer of Mehendi's personal staff, it was he who had opened the doors that permitted the mercenaries to come in. Now, he was

in an even stronger position with Okediji. Okediji
thought that he had killed Mehendi for his own
benefit.

Now, with Hendricks free, Kelo thought there was
a better than 60 percent chance that he could pull
this off again. Let your enemies do the killing for
you. If Hendricks came back, as Kelo believed he
would, it could provide the spark needed to burn out
the last of Kelo's enemies. Hendricks would come
back, and he, Kelo, would have patience and wait.
He would know what to do when the time came. He
always did.

Three miles away, in the basement of the prison,
under triple guard, the survivors of the merc strike
force waited also. Duke and Becaude shared the
same cell. Two doors away, from time to time, they
could hear a voice singing softly in German. The
sweet childlike voice belonged to the scarred and
battered face of Old Rudy the German, veteran of
Stalingrad and a dozen other smaller wars.

Duke sat in the corner of the cell on his haunches,
preferring to rest there rather than on the lice-ridden
tick mattress of his bunk. Becaude did some deep
squats, hands on hips, counting in French.

"Hey, Becaude, what do you think the boss is
doing now? He must have gotten out. From the
hell-raising that went on here and the increase in
security, he must have made it. What do you think?"

Becaude stopped after fifty, straightened up,
scratching his back. "What is there to think? If it is
possible, he will come back for us. If it is not, then
we must play our own hand. We must not just wait
for him. We must plan, and if the opportunity
presents itself, we must be ready to take it.

"The chef would not willingly leave us, but there are times when circumstance and other people prevent one from doing that which he wishes. But I know this. If the chef is free, it will take a great deal to stop him from coming back for us.

"I suspect Okediji has this problem as well as others on his mind. I would expect that he has found, even in the few days since he has taken power, that he has to deal with other nations and their opinions. He must not appear to be no more than an ignorant savage to what he will consider his peers.

"I have seen this happen more than once. I am certain that within hours of his seizing power he has had some notes of congratulation and offers of aid from some of our friends in the East. He will wish quickly to legitimatize his power in the eyes of the outside world and his neighbors.

"Even if he is completely mad, he will do this. At least for the time being. Remember Idi Amin. Even as crazy as he was, he tried to put on a good front for the rest of the world. I think that is why the executions and torture have ceased. Okediji will kill us, of that I have no doubt, but he will wait for the showcase, the trial. He would not wish for us to appear to have been excessively maltreated."

Duke scratched at his beard, found the irritation and crushed it between his nails, satisfied with the small popping sound it made.

"Maybe you're right. I hope so. This sitting around eating mealie mush with boiled cockroaches is boring."

Becaude sat on the edge of his bunk. "Not to worry, *mon vieux*. The chef will, I think, be back for us. But we must give him time. It will not be easy, and there may be those who do not wish for him to do so. It will take time. Till then, we survive, we wait and we plan."

Picking up his tin plate, Becaude examined the contents with the eye of a connoisseur. From the mealies, he selected an especially large bug, held it up to the thin light coming in from the cracks in the cell door and delicately popped it into his mouth. Smacking his lips as he looked at Duke, he said, "I have had worse."

FOUR

Major Parrish felt a sense of relief when the responsibility for Hendricks and Robbie was taken out his
hands. They, along with the boy, should now be
passing over Cairo on their way to Andrews Air
Force Base outside of Washington, D.C.

He wished them luck. From what little he had
been able to put together, he knew that Hendricks
and his young friend has been through a very rough
time. As for the rest of the mercenaries in the prison
of Bokala, the best he could wish them was quick
death.

Hendricks slept most of the way. His body needed
the healing time of sleep to reorient himself and to
prepare for the days ahead. Robbie read. Young
Collier spent his time looking out into the dark
skies, thinking about all that had happened to him
in the last few weeks. When he thought of Jan, it was
hard for him to remember what she had been like
alive. The thought of her lying on the tarmac dead,
with blood covering her face and body was the
strongest image. He had killed that night and the
next day.

The mercenaries had accepted him without prej-
udice. He had drawn the blood of those who had
killed his woman, and he wanted more of it. Like

39

Hendricks, he knew that come hell or high water those sons of bitches were not through with him. To his father over the radio he had said little, only that he was well, would fill him in when they met, and that he was returning with three other men. The men who had rescued him. He wanted his father to meet them. There was still something to be done. His father had tried to draw him out, but he would say no more.

The KC-135 settled down smoothly on the runway at Andrews. One good thing about flying military was that when you wished it, you didn't have to clear customs or answer questions. The aircraft taxied off the runway to where a line of hangars lay in wait, their bays open to accept the flights that came into Andrews from around the world.

Cutting their motors, the crew waited for the truck to be attached to their nose wheel. The plane was then pulled into the shade of an empty hangar. Once this was done, the door opened as the mobile ramp was pushed up to it. Waiting at the bottom was the reception committee, consisting of Anderson, Collier, General Forbes and Lieutenant Colonel Simpson. Behind the hangar, discreetly out of sight, was a squad of MPs, just in case there was any kind of a disturbance by the mercs.

Hendricks saw them and grunted. Behind him, Washington, Robbie and young Collier waited, speaking to no one. Hendricks thought he knew the next scenario. "They are going to try to isolate us now. Once you've gone with your father, they're going to take us away for what they call a debriefing."

"How long will that take?" Collier asked.

Hendricks smiled absently. "Who knows? Some of them have taken months, even years. That asshole Anderson, Forbes and the military will want to keep us under wraps for some time. What do you think, Robbie?"

"You're right. Unless we do something, we might just disappear into the woodwork and file cabinets."

. Anthony nodded his head, not in agreement, but thinking. Hendricks stood aside to let him go down the ramp first, to meet his father. Collier wrapped his arms around his son, fighting to keep back tears. After Anderson had filled him in, he knew how lucky he was to have his boy back alive. Anderson stood to the side, smiling broadly, benevolently. That was until Hendricks came into view with his men behind him. Anderson had already classified Robinson as a traitor. He started to move Collier and his son away to where a waiting staff car sat.

"General Forbes, you will take care of the debriefing of these other men. I will personally handle things for Mr. Collier."

As Collier and Anthony were herded toward the staff car, the boy heard Forbes give the order, and the military police squad marched through the back door into the hangar to take Hendricks and the others away.

Anthony looked back over his shoulder as the squad of MPs surrounded Hendricks and the others. It seemed as if Hendricks was right. They looked more like they were under arrest than being taken for a debriefing. Young Collier spoke quickly into his father's ear. Urgently. Anderson could see his lips moving, and the expression on Collier's face change. The emotions of the past few minutes washed away.

The concerned father was gone. In its place came the face that built a financial empire from scratch, and that had not been done by a man given to soft feelings.

Collier nodded his head once to his son, and turned to Anderson, who had a sudden sinking feeling.

"Mr. Anderson, I will be staying in Washington for a few days. I will expect to have the rest of the gentlemen, who saved my son's life, presented to me at breakfast tomorrow to thank them personally. I am certain that your General Forbes will be finished with his debriefing by that time."

Anderson swallowed deeply, embarrassed that his first words came out two octaves higher than normal.

"I am sorry, Mr. Collier, but I am positive the debriefing will take several days. . . ."

"I said tomorrow morning, at nine o'clock to be precise, and, Mr. Anderson, I am always precise. If there is any problem with this, I am certain that I can assist you in the matter with a few phone calls, which will smooth the way. It might be just as well. I haven't seen the president since our last golf game. It would do us both good to have a visit and discuss the upcoming elections."

Anderson knew he'd been had by the damn kid.

"Well, of course, Mr. Collier. Under the special circumstances, I am certain that we can arrange for Colonel Robinson to be with you at breakfast and answer your questions."

Collier's face turned to stone; Anderson saw his career diminishing into a cultural attaché post in Upper Volta.

"I said all of them, Mr. Anderson. Do it."

An order was given, not a request.

"Of course, as you say, Mr. Collier. They will be there."

"Good."

Collier got in the back seat of the staff car with his son and gave the driver his orders. The driver, like Anderson, responded to the voice of command, and he pulled way, leaving Anderson standing on the tarmac.

Looking back through the rear window, Anthony saw Anderson running into the hangar, waving his arms. Anthony smiled. Sometimes it was good to have a father like his. He had no doubt that Hendricks and the others would be with them for breakfast. But for now there was much he had to tell his father. If anything was to be done, they must have his support. He was the only one with the resources and brains to pull all the parts together quickly enough.

Collier had taken adjoining suites at the Watergate. He had been staying there for over a decade and found no reason to change, since the embarrassing events that had occurred there had nothing to do with him.

After ordering their meals brought to the rooms, young Collier started at the beginning and filled his father in on what had taken place in Bokala. As he spoke, there was a hardening about the old man's eyes and mouth. He had not come up the easy road. The first of his wealth came from wildcatting expeditions in South America and Africa. He had fought and even killed in his years. That was in the look on his face when he was told of Jan's death on the airfield. He'd had hopes for the girl. A wife for his son. He liked her, and Anthony Collier II always helped those he liked and found ways to pay off those he did not. He understood what his son meant. This was a personal thing now. A family matter, to hell with politics.

"Screw politics, Mr. Anderson, and by the way, screw you and any of these gentlemen who are with you if they choose to be involved."

Wounded, Anderson said somewhat petulantly, "Really, Mr. Hendricks, I do think that you have no idea of the sensitivity of the situation at this time. We have achieved a major international coup with the rescue of the hostages and the downfall of Mehendi. The problem is that Okediji has been fast on his feet. He has made claims that you and our people have committed murder, arson and a host of other crimes against his country. There is no doubt that at this time it is his country. According to him, you and your men fired on his without provocation and interfered with his own efforts to free the hostages at the palace. Only to save the hostages' lives did he restrain his men and permit you to take them out to the airfield. He, of course, had no idea of what your plans were at that time, but he could not let a band of obvious mercenaries simply raid his country and take out foreign nationals without any just reason. When he tried to talk to you at the airfield, your men savagely attacked him, inflicting numerous casualties on his soldiers and the civilian population."

Hendricks said, "That's bullshit and you know it."

Wearily, Anderson nodded his head. "Of course, I

know it and you know it. However, there aren't any among the hostages you rescued who say anything different. They say they know nothing about what went on between you and Okediji. However, several did state that you threatened to either kill or leave them behind if they did not do as ordered and do it fast enough. That was not a wise choice of words, Mr. Hendricks."

"How did you cover your ass on this, Anderson." Hendricks asked sourly.

"Simply enough. We said only that the plane with the hostages had to land at an airfield under American control because of engine problems. There, our forces took charge of the situation, freed the hostages from mercenary control, and returned them and the mercenaries to their respective countries."

Anderson held up a hand to stop the coming storm he knew was brewing in Hendricks. "Just a moment, let me explain, please. This was said in order to disperse your men. We said only that the plane and all involved had by chance landed in a restricted area. Therefore, from that point of view, the situation had to be handled as a security matter, and our position was that we would accept no further inquiries as to the disposition of your men or to which countries they were sent. It will all be ancient history in a few more weeks. The attention span of the public is incredibly short, Mr. H."

Anderson paced the room. It was furnished in the standard third-rate bureaucrat quasi-military fashion: steel-framed chairs, gray metal desk with waiting-room ashtrays, and very little else other than a calendar showing the faces of all the past presidents of the United States in yellowish oval frames.

Hendricks ground out a cigarette butt in the ashtray. "What about my men in prison?"

Anderson spread his hands out expressively and looked at General Forbes for moral support. Then he said, "I regret very much, Mr. Hendricks that there is absolutely nothing which we can do. We are sorry for their plight, of course. But then they did know the risks, didn't they? I am afraid that they must pay the price. But, after all, you did make a bit of a shambles of the operation. The presidential palace was nearly burned to the ground. It isn't known how many people you killed, but it was in the dozens. A veritable butcher-shop job. Bodies all over the place. We have seen photographs of the palace and the airfield. I am afraid that your associates will be tried exactly as Okediji has stated. What he does with them then is not our concern."

Hendricks kept calm. He hadn't expected anything more from them. "That's it then," he said. "We do your dirty work, then you let my people hang for it. Give me the rest of my money, so I can settle accounts. We'll call it even. As you said, we have to take our chances, don't we?"

General Forbes turned his eyes down at this. Anderson just smiled broadly. "Why, certainly, Mr. Hendricks. We shall live up to our end of the bargain. The balance of your payment will be transferred to your accounts within the week. And if I may say so, you had a bit of luck in pulling old man Collier's kid out. Be sure you thank him tomorrow because if he had not asked for it, you and the others would probably have been detained under protective custody for at least a month to let things smooth over. I am certain you can understand the reasons for that. Nothing personal, of course."

Hendricks nodded, his thin face showing nothing. This was not the time to make waves with the Americans. They were going to do nothing, which was their right, of course. He and his men were, as the phrase goes, expendable. That was what they were paid to be.

"One more thing, Mr. Anderson. What about Robinson?"

General Forbes answered, "Mr. Robinson is now a civilian. He knows of course that if he reveals anything of our nation's participation in the event, he will be charged with a breach of contract and tried. He is, as you and Mr. Washington are, free to go. When you return to your quarters, you will find a fresh change of clothing and, with Mr. Anderson's approval, five thousand dollars in cash, which will be deducted from the balance of our payment, of course."

"Of course, General, of course."

Anderson rose to signal the end of the meeting. He made a final statement. "You are free to go, Mr. Hendricks. I do hope that you show good sense and don't make any problems for us in the future, or any statements. If you do, I can promise that you will feel the full weight of the United States government's displeasure. Good-bye and good luck."

Forbes opened the door to let Hendricks out into the corridor, where two MPs were waiting to take him back to Robinson and Washington.

Their quarters were in the enclosed and secure area of Andrews. It was often used for federal pris-

oners awaiting transfer to other prisons. The rooms
were clean, and the food was the same as the airmen
ate. They could come and go from their barracks at
will, as long as they didn't cross over the warning
line next to the barbwire fences.

Washington and Robinson met him as he was
checked back in. Hendricks took them for a walk
around the compound. There were several other
guests, but those he avoided carefully. He wanted
nothing to do with them and didn't want to talk near
them. Behind the mess hall, he filled his compan-
ions in on the "debriefing" with Forbes and Anderson.

Robinson nodded his head knowingly before saying, "Sounds about right. But we seem to have a
strong ally in the boy. I did some checking while you
were away. Anthony's old man is all over the financial section of the paper. He's a hammer. If we have
any chance of getting help, it will come through
him. From what I understand, he's in tight with
everyone worth being in tight with. That's all the
way up to the top. The old man breaks them and
makes them or buys and sells them."

Hendricks looked out through the wire separating
them from the rest of the world. The monstrous
vacuum-cleaner roar of an F-16 drowned out all
sound for a few seconds till it faded in the distance.

"I don't care who we get help from," he said. "If no
one will do it we'll find a way on our own. There is
always a way if you have time, and that is what I am
afraid of. We have to find a way to buy more time."

FIVE

Kelo and Okediji both were fairly well satisfied with the progress they were making. Okediji was reducing his opposition to manageable numbers, forcing tens of thousands of Shanga tribesmen out of the country and into refugee camps. Those who remained were subject to anything—public humiliation was the least of it; death was sometimes the best of it. Property, cattle, goats, houses—they had no right to anything.

To Okediji this was only fair, for the Shanga tribesmen had done the same to his people, the Ludas, for many years. However, he would not make the mistake they had and permit too large a number of Shanga to escape into the camps outside his borders or to remain inside to breed like flies and grow powerful.

Quietly, a methodical program of extermination was taking place. Each military district commander had his quota to fill. They preferred males of any age. Women could always be absorbed. If the women had male children, then they also went to the top of the list. Leave no enemies to breed and grow strong.

Kelo was as pleased as Okediji at the slaughter of the Shanga. Let the tribesmen and butchers of Okediji do the dirty work. There would be that many less enemies when his time came. The outside world would, if he was wise, welcome his coming to power, as he would be removing yet another tyrant.

He knew how the outside world looked at Africa and knew the words he would have to use to get their aid and support. One must to outside eyes appear tolerant, democratic, just. All of these things he would be. There were other ways of dealing with the problem of excessive numbers among your enemies. Open butchery alienated those one would need later.

Okediji had made approaches to both the Soviets and Chinese with little success. In truth, Okediji was afraid to let them in. He had accepted arms from the People's Republic with the understanding that they would be paid back once he took power. The resources of his country would be the currency.

But he knew that once they or the Russians came in, he would have to dance at the end of their string. He was not a socialist or a Marxist or a communist, and he didn't want them in his country. He was the leader, he was the king, though the word was not used, and he wanted to keep it that way.

If he had had a choice, he would have preferred the People's Republic over the USSR. They were more interested in resources than influence, but he wasn't certain he could have it both ways. Since he had not lived up to his agreements with the People's Republic, the Chinese had pulled back. Still, he would try to open the door a bit, but not too far.

The Soviets had had no great success with any of their ventures on the African continent and were reluctant to place themselves on the side of another bloodthirsty maniac. World opinion was swinging

against them, and the Russians knew the value of
positive propaganda.

The other problem the Russians faced was the
difficulty in getting control over any situation in
Africa; it was simply too volatile. There were no
masses of common culture and language to deal
with. Every country had a dozen or more tribes with
different languages and different cultures, and usually they hated one another. The Russians were no
different from Germans, or Americans. They were
white, and that was reason enough not to trust them
or listen to them.

Oh, to be certain, the Africans would accept
money, guns and any kind of aid from the Russians.
But as had been proven by similar business in the
past, it would provide a poor return for the Soviets.
There was little in Bokala that the Soviets could not
acquire elsewhere at a lesser price, in money or
energy, especially now that they were trying to
reduce their costs.

They had found that subsidizing third-world re-
gimes was a costly matter, and the war in Afghani-
stan had taken hundreds of millions from their
coffers. Money which was to have gone into other
insurgent operations and maintenance programs for
their vassals in Cuba, Nicaragua and Africa.

Their only success of any degree on the dark
continent had been with Angola, and there they had
the specter of white South Africa to give them
sympathy and justification for their support of the
Marxist regime in power. That was the problem. The
regime was Marxist but only because it provided
them with the support they needed to stay in power.
They would have been happier if they could have

ruled as tribal kings, but in order to get Soviet aid, they had to be Marxists. Therefore, Marxist they were, at least as long as the aid lasted.

Kelo had no doubt that when the time came he would know how to play the proper tunes to get the maximum amount of aid from all sides. There were resources in his country yet to be developed, and he knew that without outside help they would remain that way. Too many of the African nations upon attaining independence had, in a fit of nationalism, thrown out the whites, including technicians.

This he would not do, not for some time anyway. He would have his people trained first. He would need administrators; those he would not send to Russia. Patrice Lumumba University spent more time indoctrinating and subverting its students than it did in classroom work. No. Administrators would be trained in the west, in England or the States, which he preferred.

The technicians could be sent almost anywhere they could learn to keep things such as elevators running or air conditioners working. He would need it all, however—geologists and agronomists, financial experts and trained military officers. All of this would come for his tribe, but no others, except for a token handful to keep the human rights assholes off his back.

Then, when the time was right, he would not throw out the outsiders; he would ease them out— let contracts expire and not renew them. He would make friends of all and align with none.

He knew his thinking was not modern, because he was concerned for only his own people. But that did not matter. He knew that it would be a hundred

years or more before there could be an Africa where
tribal concerns were not always paramount. Perhaps
it would never come. That did not matter either.
What did matter was today and tomorrow. The other
tribes were enemies.

This reasoning was balanced by the time Kelo had
spent in the States, studying. He knew about international thinking and civil rights. He knew about
human rights and socioeconomic relations. He
would work both sides of the street. There were
those with whom he could make alliances both in
the outside world and in his own.

There were and had been many occasions when
the different tribes and peoples of Africa worked to
each other's benefit. That was what he would do.
But first, he had to secure for his people the place of
leadership in order to be able to direct the fate and
future of the rest of the tribes.

This was what was in his mind as he crossed the
frontier where Chad and Sudan joined. His people
were waiting for him. The arms had come in. It was
time to begin to move them carefully, very carefully,
to staging areas in Bokala.

He believed that the mercenary Hendricks would
return for his men. When Hendricks returned, Kelo
would have to have some of his best men come in
early. There would be a need to instruct them very
carefully about what they were to do. He loved his
people, but like children, they were at times a bit
slow to learn.

When he crossed the border, he was on foot. He
left behind his uniform and markings of rank, changing into the rags that most of his people wore. To
wear the uniform and be alone might invite disaster.

If his tribesmen saw what they thought was an
officer from Okediji forces alone, they would probably kill him before he had a chance to identify
himself.

He walked all that night across the dry plains
where gazelle, antelope, wildebeest and elephant
once numbered in the tens of thousands. Now, he
came across only goats. A few creatures of the wild
had survived but not many. Those who had done
best were the predators, jackals and hyenas. These,
too, were being removed from the land, for they fed
upon the goats that fed upon the land and destroyed
it. Kelo knew this, but to do anything about it was a
thing far in the future.

As he walked, Kelo let his mind slip back into
childhood, when he and his father would often go for
days—not for any reason except the going—to listen
to the silence and wind. His father would tell of
what his father said, about when the rivers ran all
year and the plains were covered with grass the
height of a man's belly for as far as the eye could see.
And the animals lived, bred, hunted and died, and
there was plenty for all.

His foot hit an object and he almost lost his
balance. Looking down in the glow of the night sky,
he saw the skull of Thompson's gazelle shining stark
and white. It seemed to Kelo that it represented all
which had happened to his land. The animals first,
then the people.

At a dry wadi he came upon the rendezvous. As he
approached, he made certain that he did it in the
open, not taking cover or trying to conceal the sound
of his footsteps. He knew that he would be approached.

When he was fifty meters from their campfire, he called.

"I am here. Kelo has returned to his people."

From the brush around him figures approached, hands spread wide in greeting, their newly acquired AKs slung on their shoulders. Two detached themselves from the shadows to escort Kelo to the rendezvous, the others replaced their weapons in their hands and returned to their hiding places to guard the meeting place and those who had come.

As he came into the light of the fire, those around it rose to greet him.

"The blessings of God be upon all who have come."

His voice was steady, certain, showing nothing of the anxiety that gripped him. If this meeting failed, it would all fail. He would have to start over, and he did not know if he had the energy to do it again.

His eyes moved around the faces watching him. Two were from the Shanga tribe, former officers of Mehendi. These he had to be careful with. They knew that he had once served Mehendi and after his death was welcomed into the ranks of Okediji's Leopards. They did not trust him. But then it was not necessary that they do so. They had a common purpose—destroy Okediji. For now, they would be pliant, for Kelo was the one with the guns, and he needed some trained soldiers. Once Okediji was taken care of, Kelo would take the necessary steps to remove the former officers also.

Others present were from his tribe, the Igbo. Representatives from the Bornu, Katsin and Alafin were also there. If he could combine them, he would have the manpower to destroy Okediji and the Luda.

There was one other who sat apart: A tall, very sun-blackened man in white robes and a turban. He was part of no group. Kelo nodded slightly to him.

Moving to where the heat of the fire cast waves of blood and gold over the black of his face, Kelo began to speak to them.

"It is almost time, my brothers. Time for us to take our vengeance and regain all that has been taken from us. You know that for years I have played a loathsome role. It is true; I served with the Simbas of Mehendi, and now, after his fall, I hold high rank with the Leopards of Okediji. All of this is true. But it was through my service and patience that I brought us to this day. It was I who acquired the money to buy the weapons that are now in the hands of our young men."

He directed his next words directly at the representatives of the Shanga, who watched his every move with unblinking, hostile eyes.

"To the Shanga, I say yes, it is true. I did all that was possible to bring down Mehendi, for he was a madman. Now another madman sits in power in Bokala, and I shall bring him down also. I say to you let the past sleep, and we as one shall begin a new day. Leave the past behind and look to the dawn. Join with us and you will be, as will be the Katsin, Bornu and Igbo, a part of United Bokala. There is space and a place for all. All tribes and peoples will have a voice in the government. Each will have an autonomous homeland where they elect their leaders by their own customs, and each will have an equal voice in what will be our new congress of the people."

He moved closer to the fire. The heat was opening his pores to let sweat form and glisten on his skin.

"That is what I offer, and there is no more time for debate. To all of you I say, come with me now. Or leave, and I and my people will fight on our own. But remember this. Those who do not fight, do not share. Now, I have to return this night. You have one hour to discuss this among yourselves. I will rest and eat. I have nothing more to say. It is now for you to accept or reject. May God give you wisdom."

Kelo moved away from the campfire, back into the shadows, and the two men who escorted him in went with him. He knew them both. Another thing he knew was that if the Shanga did not align with him on this, they would never leave alive. If anyone present did not go with him, they would not leave alive. Of his people he had no doubts. They were his. But he could not take the chance that any of the others would leave and then betray him to Okediji. That was too great a risk. At this meeting only his men were armed, and they were loyal only to him.

He whispered in the ear of one of the sentries. The man smiled, and even in the dark his teeth showed great and white. He had little love for the Shanga. As the sentry moved to give the orders to the other guards around the meeting place, he hoped that Kelo would order them to kill the Shanga.

Food was brought to Kelo. He didn't taste it and, after eating, could not recall what it was. His mind was on those at the campfire who had at first drawn into their separate groups by tribe and were now meeting all together. He checked his watch: ten minutes to go, then it would be done.

He saw them all stand facing toward him in the

dark. The wind blew lightly in his direction. He could smell the smoke and oil of their bodies and the dust, from the dry land, that settled deep into their pores. He rose slowly and walked back to them.

Very slowly he looked at their faces and knew he had won. Only the Shanga were sullen, but their expressions said that they, too, accepted his terms. What choice did they really have?

Kelo did not wait for them to give him their decision. He spoke first.

"Good, my brothers. I see we are in agreement. Now, this is what you shall do. The Bornu will move their men to camp by the two valleys and there wait for my word to cross into Bokala. This they will do in small groups of three and four. You of the Katsin and Alafin will cross from Chad in the same manner. My people, the Igbo, most of them are in Bokala now. They will await their orders. To you of the Shanga, you will cross from your refugee camps. Again, move in small groups and gather at the river crossing of Borku."

He stopped any questions with "There will be no arms until you have moved our warriors to their gathering places inside Bokala. When they are there, you will find the weapons waiting for you. All that I have promised is a fact. To that effect I invite you to speak to Ibn Malik."

He signaled for the man in the white robes to come forth from the shadows. All knew his name. Ibn Malik, a Sudanese, was well known for his dealing in arms throughout central and eastern Africa.

"*Salaam aliekum*, Ibn Malik," Kelo said. "You will please inform my brothers of the business we have done that they may have confidence in my words."

Malik moved to the fire, crossing his arms under his robes. He spoke so softly that the others had to strain to hear his words. He spoke in that manner because of the scar across his throat, where a knife had tried to reach his jugular and failed.

"It is true," he began. "I swear it by the holy Koran and prophet Mohammed, blessed be his name, that Kelo *effendi* has made a large purchase of weapons from me. At his disposal there are five thousand of the AK-47 rifles made by the infidel Russians and purchased from the Palestinians. There are one hundred and fifty light machine guns, fifty mortars of different calibers and the shoulder rockets RPG-7, of which there are two hundred. Of ammunition, it is in abundance. All of these have I delivered and been paid for. They are now in the possession of Kelo *effendi*." Having finished what he had to say, Malik salaamed and moved back into the shadows.

Those present believed him. Ibn Malik was a man to inspire confidence and faith. Jalingo Kelo had the guns, and they would do his bidding.

SIX

On the following morning Hendricks, Robinson and Washington were taken in an unmarked staff car to the Watergate, as Anderson had promised Collier. With them they took the few personal possessions issued at the base. Toothbrushes and money, that was it.

They were escorted by an Air Force staff sergeant as far as the door to Collier's suite. As soon as the door opened in response to their knock, the sergeant left without looking back. He didn't know why he was supposed to take them there. He didn't know who they were and knew better than to ask.

The elder Collier stood in the doorway and waited with a secretive smile on his face.

"Please come in, Mr. Hendricks, you and your associates." Collier was always careful to use exact wording when possible. He didn't know if the men in the doorway classified each other as friends or not. Associates in some form they certainly were.

He ushered them into the best the hotel had to offer, a richly furnished, large living room with a stocked bar and two connecting bedrooms. Hendricks figured it cost in the area of six hundred dollars a night. But then for Collier, it was probably tax deductible.

Breakfast waited on a side bar, under sterling silver domes, kept warm by the flames of small gas burners.

"If you are hungry, gentlemen, please serve yourselves. I have already eaten, so do not let me deter you."

Hendricks moved to the table with Washington and Robinson. For himself he took only coffee; Robinson and Washington helped themselves to large portions of eggs Benedict with Canadian ham. Collier picked a seat across from Hendricks, so he could watch the man's face and movements. You could very often tell more about a person by his body language than you could by his words.

Robinson and Washington were content to enjoy the food. They knew that at this moment they had little to contribute. They would be asked if they were needed to give any additional input. But for now, this was between Hendricks and the two Colliers.

Anthony provided the ice breaker by saying, "I have told my father about what happened. All of it as far I know. Of course, I don't know anything about who, as you say, contracted you, though after yesterday I have a pretty good idea. The important thing is, if you can justify your proposed actions, my father is willing to listen and possibly commit to aiding us in the matter."

Hendricks liked it when Anthony said, "us." The boy was daily gaining more merit in his eyes. Anthony had the makings of a tough son of a bitch, and Hendricks liked the looks of the old man. There were lines in his face that came from living, not good food and wine. His hands were wrapped around

the delicate handle of a china coffee cup and looked
as if they'd have been more at home on an oil rig or
a ripsaw. Both of which, he knew, the old man was
personally familiar with.

The questions and answers began. Hendricks
knew he would have to give Collier all of it, the good
and bad; and he did, from start to end, until Collier
had it all. When they finished, Collier leaned back,
poured a cup of black coffee, wrapped his large
workman's hands around the cup and nodded his
head.

"Very well, Mr. Hendricks. I believe what you say,
and I know from my son that everything you have
told me from the moment you picked him and his
girl up on the street is correct. Before I commit
myself one way or the other, I would like for you to
know the reasons for my decision."

Setting the thin-shelled cup on the table, Collier
leaned back in his chair and ran his thick fingers
through his grey, carefully trimmed hair. His eyes
were very blue and hard, except when he talked
about his son; then there was a slight thaw. Not
much but it was there.

"Very well, Mr. Hendricks. Might I call you Martin? I understand that is your first name, and under
these circumstances, I think we might forego excessive formality. Do you agree?"

"Certainly, Mr. Collier." Collier made no com-
ment about Hendricks's continued use of mister,
because he knew it would be confusing if Hendricks
addressed both him and his son as Anthony.

"Good, then to continue. My son has told me that
during your time in the prison at Bokala he filled
you in on much of his life and of mine.

"As that is the case, you know that I came up the hard way and am damned proud of it. Everything I have, I made myself. And in the doing, I had to run over a few bodies. I do not like being pushed around or threatened. I do not like my people, and especially members of my family, to be pushed around.

"The only thing I probably dislike more is people who let themselves be pushed around. My son has said that he is going back with you come hell or high water. I like that. A man who doesn't believe in settling accounts wouldn't be worth a shit in running an empire."

Hendricks began to feel much better about the possibility of Collier giving them support.

"Martin, Anthony is my only son. You saved him once. For that I owe you. Why you did it does not matter in the slightest. You did it, and that means I have a debt to pay to you. Now, he says he wants to go back with you. I understand that if he does he might well be killed. If he is, then that was his choice. I will hold no one else responsible. A man has to take his chances.

"But we, as survivors—and I think we both classify as that—know that good planning, preparation and money often make the difference between success and failure. I do not like failure in myself, and I will not like it in any venture in which my son is involved.

"Therefore, bring me a plan. Bring me an idea of what is required. If I agree, you will have my unstinted support. And I assure you, Martin, it is considerable."

Hendricks stood up, walked around the table and extended his hand, saying, "I think we'll get along fine, Mr. Collier. I know now where your son gets his balls."

In spite of himself, Collier was pleased. His son was his vanity, though not his only one.

"First we need intel on what's taking place, and we need to find a way to keep my men in as good a shape as possible. When the time comes to take them out, the healthier they are the easier it'll be. If any of you have any ideas," he addressed everyone, "I'm ready to listen."

There was silence as the men looked around at each other for a few moments. Then Washington spoke up.

"I got an idea, Boss, but it might sound a bit strange."

"Go ahead, Washington, sometimes strange works."

Washington pushed his plate away and sat back, taking time to find the right words.

"Okay, you know but maybe the others don't. I was born in that part of the world but was raised in the States. I think I might have a bit more insight into the mind of someone like Okediji. My little brother was a 'return to Africa' and *Roots* nut. A lot of what I picked up was through him. It was the same input, but I interpreted it differently from him because he wasn't born there."

Washington stood to move beside Hendricks. "Okay, this is it, Boss. Anthony said that his daddy here was the equivalent of big time bucks in all kinds of things and one of those things was in movies. Is that right, Mr. Collier?"

Collier answered with interest, "Yes, it is Mr. Washington. I do hold a major interest in a film production company."

"Good, then this is the idea. Understand, Boss, that men like Okediji and Mehendi think of themselves as being the next best thing if not better than God. They live on ego and conceit. A cameraman is never far away. Remember Idi Amin, he lived with a camera up his asshole."

Washington paused theatrically.

Hendricks and Collier both spoke at the same time. "Go on!"

"Well I've been thinking about this for a couple of days, even on the flight over, when me and Anthony shared a few thoughts. It's this. We do a movie based on the life and times of Leopoldo Okediji."

There was silence. Washington didn't want to lose the initiative. "I'm serious, guys. Listen to me. We use Mr. Collier's company as a front. Everyone loves the movies. We go in, meet with Okediji, tell him we want to film his life story, a major production. That will give us a chance to maybe get close to our guys and find out what's happening to them."

Collier stood up to join them, a gleam coming to his eye. He thought he knew where Washington was taking them. "And just who will go meet with Leopoldo Okediji?" he asked.

Washington grinned slyly. "Why me, of course. At this time, I think it would be pretty tough for a honky to get very close to him.

"Now that we've escaped, he's going to be pretty touchy about white folks. I'm the only black face you got."

There was some discussion for the next three hours. Lunch was brought in, half eaten and forgotten. Collier found himself becoming involved with the idea. It was a bit wild, but it might work.

He said to the gathering, "I didn't expect action this fast. But if this will start the ball rolling, I'll go along with it. I can see that Mr. Washington has the proper credentials and credits.

"But he will need a history. There is a black producer who's popular with the underground and soul-searching types, who has done some films in New York. He is known to be a strong black activist, civil rights advocate and very vocal opponent of apartheid. In fact, he is an opponent of every color, except his own and the color of money.

"I think we might be able to buy his identity for a time. We can move Mr. Washington to L.A.; there he will be given an office in my studio, phones, addresses, secretaries, the whole thing. We'll even assign a scriptwriter to him."

Extending his rough paw, Collier said sincerely, "Mr. Washington, you have just become a movie producer with a big budget to do a socially relevant film about the life and times of Leopoldo Okediji."

Washington thought he liked the sound of that. "Right on. I can play that part. Shit, us blacks have been playing different roles all our lives. All I need is the threads and the money."

Collier smiled at him tolerantly. "You will also need to know a bit of the dialogue used out there. I will have Jameson find someone to tutor you in it. He will also bring you some literature to read. You know, books such as *The Producer's Guide to Filmmaking, Directing and Casting.*

"But the best thing you will have on your side is me and my son. If you don't talk too much, the people out there won't know the difference. Be vague, and they'll think you're artistic, not ignorant.

At any rate, you have a couple of days to prepare. Use that time well, Mr. Washington; use it well. I do not like people who fail me. If you think Mr. Hendricks is bad, then you nappy-headed hustler, you ain't seen nothing yet."

Washington was shocked at the words that came out of the old man's mouth, he was just too decent and rich looking. Then Washington remembered the way Collier had made his money.

"Right. I read you. No mistake, sir. And I won't mess up. I'll do just what I'm supposed to."

SEVEN

Hendricks and Robinson began their own operations planning. No matter what else was done, they were going to need weapons and men—good men, tough men. As long as they had the money, they knew there would be no great difficulty in acquiring either.

Collier did as he had promised. He turned the job over to Jameson, who found the low-budget, black director-writer-producer Mr. Malcolm Jones living in a cold-water flat in the Village.

Jameson offered him a contract to write a script based on the inequities of apartheid in South Africa, a strong adventure script with big screen potential.

To make things easier for Mr. Jones, Jameson also gave him a house in Chiapas, Mexico, where he and his girl friend could live and work without the interruptions of the city. It was a remote house without phone service but fully staffed with servants, who would see to their needs and privacy.

Part of the servants' instructions was to see that no one disturbed or bothered them. The need for secrecy was stressed to Mr. Jones, who knew quite well that there were people who would prefer not to see a production of this nature ever get off the ground. He had to agree, therefore, to complete the script in secrecy if he was to get the contract. There was also a very strong possibility that he might be given the opportunity to direct the film.

Jameson suggested that Jones be ready in the event that he had to go out of the country to do research. To this end, he arranged for Jones to have his passport photos taken that afternoon. Jameson also had Jones fill out the application for a passport, which he had brought with him. Jones had a copy of his birth certificate, which expedited matters. Mr. Jameson said it would take a couple of weeks to get the passport but not to worry, he would take care of everything.

Malcolm was a bit suspicious until Jameson suggested he call the studio head in L.A. collect. He did. The president of the studio said that Mr. Jameson was empowered to make whatever arrangements or financial agreements he thought were right. The studio was subject to his orders, and they were looking forward to the opportunity to work with a rising talent such as Jones.

Malcolm Jones and his girl friend, a part-time nude model-dancer, were on a plane for Mexico the following evening. The ten thousand advance for the film treatment felt very comfortable in his pocket. The white dude had even paid off his rent and taken a list of the people he owed money to, promised to take care of them, tell them that he had a writing assignment and would be out of the city for a time. In fact, Jameson informed those he met that Jones was going to California.

Mr. Jones felt very well indeed. He knew that his time had come. He didn't know who his financial angel was, and he didn't care. But the man was definitely organized.

He smiled at the strong young Latin sitting across from him in first class. When Jones said he didn't speak Spanish, Mr. Jameson had this Latin type, named Arnoldo something or other, assigned to him as an interpreter and research assistant.

The dude could type, take shorthand and do all kinds of useful things. He knew his place, too. Always called him sir and his woman miss. The sucker was fast with a cigarette lighter and everything else. He tried to anticipate Jones's needs and was always close when he was needed.

No, he didn't care who the angel was. Jameson was a heavy-time man, but Jones had the feeling that there was someone even stronger behind him. No matter, he'd find out soon enough. For now it was good just to know that his time had come. He'd been recognized, and now he would be able to do things and do them his way. This was his opportunity to break into the big time.

Hendricks was amazed at how fast Collier could get things done. Funds had been arranged for him through Collier's bank in Belgium, which had branch offices in the Bahamas. Washington was already on his way to L.A., where a staff would be waiting to follow his orders.

Jameson went with Washington to the passport agency's main office in D.C. With the juice of Collier's office, there were no difficulties in having a passport issued the same day in the name of Mr. Malcolm Jones but with Washington's picture.

The next two days were spent firming up Washington's ID, rearranging financing and going over options. Hendricks had two more meeting with Old Man Collier. Each time he liked him more. The man was wealthy as few ever dream of being, but it didn't really mean shit to him. At his age, the numbers were only a mark by which he graded himself. The money itself was nothing. It was only a tool, and tools were designed to be used. That was all it meant to him. A tool to help his son do something that was important to him. He told Hendricks something that helped him to understand better his motivations.

"Mr. Hendricks, I know that you probably think I'm a bit mad to even consider what we are doing. But I believe in madness. Both kinds. There are forms of madness that a man must go through to prove himself. It can come in many forms. My son, as you know, is not a pussy. But then neither has he, with the exception of his time with you, been really tested. It's not me who needs the proving, it's him. If he can do one mad thing in life and win, if he can prove his courage and intelligence to himself, then he's a made man with or without my money. I can buy physical things, but I cannot purchase one ounce of courage. Courage is something that my son must have if he is to be a man in his own eyes.

"He thinks he has had it too soft and must show me that he can be tough, too. I don't need that proof, but he does. Therefore, I am going along with you on this to the limit. You don't gamble with scared money."

Hendricks nodded in understanding. He had his own form of madness to live with, or he wouldn't be doing the things he did. There was a place for the mad in the world, without whom everything would only be a dull shade of gray.

He told Collier, "I think I know what you mean. But even if you're willing to do so, I have to carry more than my own body weight in this. I have enough put away to be able to cover some of the costs involved. The weapons and military gear, I can access and pay for. Also it keeps you out of the illegal gun business. By the way, what's going to happen to you and Anthony even if we do pull it off? A lot of people are going to be very pissed, and it is illegal. There could be a dozen different charges against you, including murder, before this is done. And there will be no way to do this without people dying."

Collier only smiled at him, his face stretching into deep lines and crevices.

"Me, Hendricks? Money can buy many things, it can even buy immunities to a degree. If we were going into a nice gentle land to do this, I couldn't cover it. There I think I can. If I can't, then the only response I can think to accurately describe the situation and the possible charges against me and mine is screw it! If you're afraid to play, get out of the game. In fact, don't even think about getting in it to begin with. You go and cover what you have to, and I'll cover things here. Mr. Hendricks, we are going into the movie business in a way that's never been done before."

Hendricks and Robinson made reservations to go to Guatemala. There, at Hendricks's home, he would be able to call in a few favors. He needed weapons and didn't have time to go through normal channels.

But in Guatemala, at the cuartel general army post
at Rufios Barrios, there was a warehouse filled with
surplus arms that the Guatemalan army no longer
used. Most of them were out of date, WWII issue.
Old but functional. Thompson smgs, M3s, BARs and
.30 Browning lmgs, enough to outfit a couple of
battalions, but he only needed arms and ammo for
fifty.

He'd been through the warehouse before, when he
picked out some rifles for the sniper training course
he had run for the Ejercito last year.

Through a friend with a class-three importer's
license in Atlanta, he'd arranged a front to purchase
the arms. No end user certificate was required, but
the arms had to be sold to a licensed dealer from
somewhere to meet the Guate legal requirements.

The only difference was that the arms would
never enter the States, and Guatemalans didn't care
where they went as long as they didn't end up in
Central America in the wrong hands.

Hendricks knew they would probably suspect he
was up to something, but he had been a good friend
to them at a time when they had been short of
friends. He felt they would not question him too
closely on the matter.

He would arrange for them to be paid for the arms
in cash. Then they would be sent to Puerto Barrios
on the Caribbean side of the country, loaded on a
small coastal freighter and taken out to sea. From
there they would be met by a seaplane and taken to
a trans-shipment point in the Bahamas to be stored,
ready for when they would be needed.

When they cleared customs at Aurora International Airport and hit the street, it was like coming home for Hendricks.

Flagging down a cab, he gave the address for Don Quijote's in zone one. He'd go there first and use the phone to contact Antonio Sarda.

Tono had been his principal contact in Guatemala for the last three years. If anyone could get him into see General Ponce fast, it would be him. The man had more lines out than a tuna boat.

Paying off the driver of the rattling wreck of a cab with a twenty quetzal bill, he and Robbie took their bags out of the trunk and entered the Quijote, leaving the noise of the street outside where it belonged.

Dario, the Spanish owner, was chewing out Carlos the headwaiter, for taking off on a three-week drunk. Carlos, an ex-boxer, had the look of a whipped puppy as Dario verbally worked him over. A shy grin of relief came over his face as he saw Hendricks enter; he was going to be given a temporary reprieve. Dario saw them a second after Carlos did.

"Ola compadre. Uno para la corazon!" he asked, as he always did when Hendricks came in, touching his chest.

Hendricks smiled. "Yes, Dario, give me one for the heart. I need it."

Dario poured a stiff Johnny Walker and looked with open curiosity at Robbie. "Something for your friend, Marteen?"

Robbie looked questioningly at Hendricks, who shrugged. "They don't have any bourbon here, better try the beer. Give him a Gallo, Dario, and can I use the phone?"

"Por su puesto amigo!"

Dario pulled the phone out from under the bar and handed it to him.

Hendricks dialed Tono's number and waited for the ring, looking around the Quijote. It was good to be back among familiar things and people. Nothing had changed. The walls were still decorated with posters of bullfights and not much else. Dario had a ninety percent Spanish clientele; the rest were mixed gringos and Europeans. The food was good, the prices reasonable and the beer always cold.

A woman's voice answered on the other end of the line. *"Ministeria de la Defensa."*

"Señor Antonio Sarda, por favor."

"Momento."

It took a little longer than a moment for the familiar voice to come on the line.

"Tono, Martin here. I'm back and need to see you soon. I need some help."

Tono wasted no time on small talk. If Martin needed help, then it was important.

"Right. Where are you?"

"I just got in and I'm at the Quijote."

"Good, wait there. I'll be over in fifteen minutes."

As Hendricks hung up, Carlos came over to greet him. Built like one of the short, stocky Spanish fighting bulls in the posters, he hugged Hendricks around the shoulders.

"You been a bad boy again, Carlos?"

Carlos shrugged his heavy shoulders eloquently, smiled and spread his hands. That was all he had to say.

"All right, you bleedin' little sod. Put our bags behind the bar, okay?"

EIGHT

Hendricks motioned for Robbie to join him at the table in the corner under a bullfight poster promoting Paco Camino, an old poster.

Robbie set his bottle, with the red rooster on the label, down, saying, "Good beer. You reach your friend?"

Hendricks nodded, "Yes, he'll be here in a few minutes. So we might as well take it easy. I'll call my house after we talk to Tono. Until we do that, I won't know which switch to pull."

Robbie had just ordered his second beer when Tono came in, as always looking as if he were dressed to do a men's clothing commercial. Tono was tall, with dark eyes and short roman-cut hair. His nose was slightly crooked; the cops in Mexico had given him the seltzer water treatment eight years ago when he'd been caught trying to bring a load of guns through Mexico to Guatemala.

He and Hendricks embraced in the Latin fashion. Hendricks introduced Robbie to him, saying, "He was with me on the last contract."

Tono ordered an aqua mineral with lemon. He had quit drinking five years earlier.

"All right, Martin, what is it?"

Hendricks filled him in on the events of the last

few weeks and what he needed. Tono was sympathetic. He knew not only Martin, but Duke and Becaude as well, and he liked them all.

"Weapons, I see. And you think that Ponce can help you get them out of the surplus arms bodega? Perhaps so. He likes you and remembers you with fondness. He asks often about you. I'll call him now and see when we can get an appointment. If he can help I am sure that he will, but it will have to be handled very quietly and very delicately. We don't want the rest of the world screaming that we are selling arms to *mercenaries*, forgive the expression."

"Nothing to forgive, Tono. It's accurate enough."

Tono took the phone, turned his back to the bar and dialed a number. When a voice answered on the other end of the line, he spoke rapidly with authority and paused. Then Hendricks heard him say, *"Mi General."*

The rest of the conversation was too fast and muted for Hendricks to follow. Tono spoke not only with his mouth but in the Latin fashion with his hands. Once you learned how to read his hand language, you could at least get an idea of how the conversation was going.

Having put the receiver back down, he joined Robbie and Hendricks at the table.

"Okay, this is it. You can see the general at six this evening. That is in one hour and fifteen minutes."

"Thanks, Tono. Can you go with us? Sometimes my Spanish is a little rough, and I don't want any mistakes when I talk to him. This has to be made very clear."

Tono got up, straightening a nonexistent wrinkle in his jacket.

"Of course. I'll come for you at ten minutes to six. I have a few things yet to do at the National Palace."

Turning to Robbie, he extended his hand. "A pleasure to meet you, Colonel Robinson."

"Just Robbie will do. I'm not in the service any longer. As Martin told you, I am now among the retired and unemployed."

Tono smiled. "Do not let that concern you unduly. I am sure with mine and Martin's help you can find a consultant's position with our own air force. They are in need of some good advisors. Our pilots are very brave and dedicated, but since the Carter years, they are bit behind on current techniques and training."

Robbie let loose of Tono's hand. "Sounds like a plan to me. Thank you, Mr. Sarda."

"Just call me Tono. For I think we shall in time become great friends. That is if you live long enough. Hanging around my friend here has been known to make life insurance actuaries very nervous."

Stepping back, Tono, through force of habit, adjusted the concealed Smith and Wesson Model 59 riding on his hip under his jacket.

"Very well, I would like to stay, but I do have business to take care of. Till later, then, gentlemen."

Hendricks called his home in the hills outside of Gaute City. Tino Garcia, his gardener and house guard, an ex–national policeman, answered. Hendricks spoke for a few minutes, said *"hasta despues"* and hung up.

"Okay, at least we'll have something to eat when we get home, Robbie."

Robbie nodded his head between swallows of the Gallo.

"Better ease up on that. I want you with us when we meet General Ponce."

"Right," Robbie set the bottle down. "Then what about some chow?"

Hendricks motioned with his finger for Carlos to bring them a menu. A few words and Carlos left to prepare them a dish of freshwater *camarónes* in garlic and butter.

It was nearly time for them to meet again with Tono when they had cleaned off their plates.

Hendricks led the way to the street, stopping at the entrance to Quijote's, where they were assailed by the noise and diesel fumes of passing buses, trucks with no mufflers, and the distant whining of an ambulance siren. Looking to his left past the Bank of America, Hendricks saw a couple of jeeps with .30-caliber mgs mounted on them go by in the direction of the National Palace.

While he'd been gone, there had been another coup attempt, but it involved only a few units of the army. The rest remained loyal to the new president, or, if not the new president, they remained loyal to the generals who supported him. They wanted no more *golpes*. It was bad for the economy, bad for foreign relations and bad for the tourist business. They were trying to break the pattern, but it wasn't easy.

General Otto Ponce had been the main man who stopped the coup before it literally got started. Most of the dissident commanders came from the south coast, where he had recently been a commander. They knew him and didn't want to screw with him.

He met them with a few troops from general headquarters at kilometer twenty-one outside the city
and told them that if they wanted a fight, it would
begin there. The dissident commanders took their
troops back to the barracks.

Hendricks heard a blast from an air horn and saw
Tono pulling around the corner in a Jeep Cherokee
with dark tinted windows to keep curious eyes from
seeing who was inside. Usually big shots had their
vehicles done over in this manner. It had been
popular in El Salvador until the guerrillas started
shooting up every vehicle with dark windows no
matter who was in them.

Hendricks got in the front seat with Tono; Robbie
got in the back. Heading down Eleventh Calle, they
drove over to zone six, making twists and turns past
churches half-wrecked from the last earthquake and
years of neglect. There was some restoration work
going on—tourists love colorful old churches; re-
storing them was good for business, and Guatemala
was becoming very business oriented.

Military traffic picked up as they turned down the
narrow street leading to the main entrance of the
cuartel general. They were waved on through an
intersection by a couple of PMA with Galil assault
rifles on their backs. Policia Militar Ambulante also
came under the command of Ponce.

At the gate, a *teniente* came over to the jeep. He
knew the vehicle, but he still checked on the passengers and asked to see Tono's ID. Then he returned to the guard house, made a quick call, bobbed
his head, saluted the phone and waved them
through.

Tono parked the vehicle by the Officers Club and

led them through the entrance to the interior of the old fort. They were checked in by security, and a corporal was assigned to escort them to the general's office.

General Ponce was with someone else at the time. The guard indicated for them to take seats on a bench outside the office. Hendricks walked over to a rampart and looked out at the city below. The lights were coming on as the sky darkened. He liked the old fort. It had the feel of time to it, not something sterile like so many army posts around the world.

On the left hand side facing Ponce's door was an old, water-cooled .30-caliber Browning. On the right was something most collectors would kill for: a Gatling gun with the original carriage, a .58-caliber made in 1867. Hendricks wondered what actions it had been in and where. The Gatling surprised most people who visited the offices of the HQ. Not him—he had been in their warehouse more than once. Inside he'd seen weapons that belonged in museums, lying in stacks, untended and decaying.

Tono called to him, saying, "We can go in now."

Turning, Hendricks saw two men in business suits going back the way the three of them had come in. The same guard who had escorted them in was taking the men in business suits out.

Ponce came to the open door to greet them. His smile was genuine. At first glance, if he'd been in civies, you might have thought him a pleasant businessman, until you noticed his bearing and manner. He was a man who was comfortable with authority. He wore it well but not in an overbearing manner. He was in his early fifties, around five nine, a hundred forty-five well conditioned pounds, thinning hair, with a mustache and sharp intelligent eyes. He had eliminated most of Guatemala's guerrilla problems on the south coast when he had been commander there.

He greeted Hendricks and Tono warmly in Spanish. He understood more English than he spoke. Tono introduced Robinson with his military rank, which was the custom here even if you were no longer in the service. Titles were very important. They put a person in a category that could be registered and gave the person an instant identity.

Ushering them inside, Ponce showed them to a well-worn and comfortable leather couch and chairs. The office was Spartan. In one corner leaned a Mexican Mendoza light machine gun, a gift from one of Ponce's Mexican contemporaries. Behind the desk was the blue and white Guatemalan flag. On the walls were a collection of photographs of past commanders of the general headquarters. Some of the faces were pure Indian. Eyes long dead could still stare you down if you looked at them too long.

Most of the commanders of the cuartel general went on to become either minister of defense or in some cases something even higher. However, that would not be the case with General Ponce. He had no political ambitions. Soldiering was what he did and what he wanted to do. The intrigues of Central American political life did not much interest him. He would leave that to other, more ambitious men. He was content.

NINE

Letting them get settled, Ponce had an orderly bring coffee. Then he waited till cups were tasted before beginning in Spanish, which left Robbie out of most of it.

"How may I be of service, my friend? Tono tells me you have a problem."

Hendricks repeated, he thought for the hundredth time, the story of the raid and rescue. Ponce clucked his lips in both sympathy and admiration.

Then, after Hendricks had finished, he said, "You want some of my old guns to go back in and get your men out. Is that correct?"

Hendricks nodded. "Yes, sir. I need weapons fast, and it would take too long to go through other channels. I am certain the Americans have put the word out to stay away from me. They can lean pretty heavy when they want to."

Ponce sipped at his cup. "That is true enough, but here in Guatemala, we do pretty much as we please. The Americans did not aid us very much in the last years when we needed it. Though in a way, I think this has had a positive effect. We have shown that we can deal with our own problems without American aid when we have to. But back to your problem . . ."

Putting the cup back on the saucer, he stood up. "Come with me. I want to show you something."

He called to the rear room. Major Castillo, a short, barrel-chested man, came in, snapped to attention and barked crisply, "*Si, mi General.*"

"Bring the keys to the bodega," Ponce ordered.

"*A su ordenas, mi General.*" Castillo stamped his right foot, did an about face left and was back in five seconds with a ring of keys.

"Please come with me." He led the way out into the inner compound, up a small incline between gray painted barracks and storerooms, till they were in front of what had used to be the old magazines for the fort. Ponce indicated one of the three doors that faced him, and Castillo unlocked the padlock and stood to the side.

"You will wait here, Major Castillo."

He motioned for the rest of them to follow him down the stairs into a musty corridor lined with weapons of every vintage and caliber. Spanish 7mm mausers rested beside .03 Springfields, Enfields and Czech ZB24s. Taking them past a pile of a couple hundred German MP40s, Ponce opened a side door, reached inside and turned on the light.

Hendricks went in first, followed by Robinson and Sarda. Robbie heard Hendricks whistle.

Ponce smiled broadly as he waved his hand around the room. "These are confiscated weapons. A month ago our navy people brought in a coastal trader with this contraband. It was on its way to Colombia, a shipment for the drug dealers. I think it might serve you better than what you requested, and it will be easier for me to dispose of, because as contraband it is not listed on our military inventory."

The room was stacked with crates of new Belgium-manufactured FALs, MAG light machine guns. Mixed with them was a variety of modern weapons, some Uzis and HK MP5s, a half dozen 60mm mortars, boxes of grenades and two recoilless rifles of the 57mm caliber. Ammo manufactured in Yugoslavia was stacked in crates to the ceiling. There was enough to outfit an infantry battalion and do it damned well.

Ponce was pleased at Hendricks's reaction. "Do you think any of this will help?" He knew it would.

Hendricks just shook his head. "My General, if you can arrange for me to get some of this equipment, I don't know how I will ever repay you."

Ponce laughed pleasantly. "No problem. I know how. You need enough equipment for fifty men. I will give you whatever you need from here, including ammunition. You will pay for this in medical supplies. My people are very short of such things as battle dressings, morphine and antibiotics. For these weapons and ammunition, you will give me one hundred thousand dollars' value in medical supplies.

"In addition, I will have them delivered by the army to Puerto Barrios on the coast. There will be no bill of lading and no documentation on them. These weapons do not exist. Unfortunately, the ten men of the contraband ship were killed when they tried to escape military custody. They were the only ones who knew the contents of the ship."

Hendricks asked him, "When did this happen?"

General Ponce grinned at him before answering. "Tomorrow morning."

For the next hour Ponce left Hendricks alone in the warehouse with Robinson. Antonio excused himself, saying he had a late meeting at the Residencia with the minister of finance and the minister of defense. Ponce returned to his office, leaving Major Castillo at the door of the bodega to attend Hendricks and Robbie if they needed it.

Robinson was dumbfounded at some of the confiscated weapons hanging on racks at the rear of the warehouse. Artillery Lugers and WWII P-38s were mixed in with Colt single sixes a hundred years old. Over two thousand pistols hung by their trigger guards from steel rods running the length of the wall and rising in layers to the ceiling.

"Jesus Christ," Robbie exclaimed, "this shit belongs in a museum! You know there is a Lemot hanging there! The last one I heard of sold at auction for over six thousand dollars!"

Hendricks laughed. "Yes, I know. But the law here is very strange. They can confiscate, but there is nothing on the books that permits them to dispose of confiscated weapons. Some of those have been hanging there for a hundred years."

It took three hours for Hendricks to check out the weapons he wanted and to move them to one side of the bodega. He chose two 60mm mortars with a hundred rounds of high explosive and Willy Peter shells, fifty FALs with ten mags each, twenty Uzis with six mags each and five MAG lmgs.

He wanted every man to have at least a double basic load and then some, for there wouldn't be any resupply where they were going. He topped it off with five cases of hand grenades, the three-second toss-and-pop variety.

When they had finished and left the bodega with Major Castillo, it was nearly eleven. Ponce had left

the post, but Castillo had orders to provide them
with transport. A brown Chevy Citation with a
driver in civilian clothes waited for them by the
motor pool.

"Thank you, Major," Hendricks said. "I appreciate
your patience."   .

Castillo responded politely without smiling. *Por
nada, señor.*

Hendricks and Robinson got in the back for the
ride up to Hendricks's home, in the mountains
between Guatemala City and Antigua, a half hour's
ride that went up another thousand feet over the five
thousand–plus altitude of the city.

The night was cool, and Hendricks was glad to
finally be going home, where he could think. The
driver took the short way over Jumper's Bridge, so
called because of the number of suicides made from
it each year. It was a common joke that bridge
jumping was going to be Guatemala's entry in the
next Olympics. From there they turned onto
Avenida Roosevelt, which would take them out of
town on CA1 past Mixco and on into the mountains.
Past Mixco you could feel the temperature drop ten
degrees in five minutes.

There was little conversation on the way up. They
were both tired. Hendricks hadn't expected to be
able to get in and see Ponce this fast, much less get
into the warehouse and start picking out equipment.
Maybe it was a good sign.

The driver left them off in front of the gate. Tino
was waiting for them. He opened the gate, welcoming the *jefe* back home. A Galil on his shoulder, he'd
been walking his rounds.

Tino's wife, Alejandra, did most of Hendricks's

cleaning and laundry. His five children ranged from six months to ten years and were usually somewhere on the grounds during the day, if Hendricks did not have company or was not involved with business. The first finger on both of Tino's hands was shorter than the others. Machete fights had trimmed them down.

Hendricks smelled wood smoke. Here in the mountains it was cool if not cold at nights. Tino had built a fire to warm the house before his arrival. Taking their bags, he followed after Hendricks and Robinson. Once inside the house, he took Robinson's bags to the guest room and put a fire on under the coffee pot.

He could see by Hendricks's eyes that things were not well. He didn't ask what was wrong. If the *jefe* wanted him to know, he'd tell him. If not, then it was the *jefe*'s business, not his. His job was to take care of the house, the things in it, the garden and fruit trees. Good work and also he was trusted, and that meant a great deal to him. There was no need to steel anything from the *jefe*. If Hendricks knew his family needed something, it was forthcoming.

Now Tino knew the *jefe* and his guest needed to rest. Throwing a few more logs on the fire, he asked if there was anything else he would be needed for.

"No, Tino. That's all for the night. Thank you. I'll see you in the morning."

Robinson was tired. It had been a long day, and the mental aggravation was as bad as the physical. It would be good to lay the body down between cool, crisp sheets for a while.

"Look, Boss, I'm going to put it down for a while. If you need me, just knock. I'm a light sleeper."

Hendricks smiled wearily at him, saying "Aren't we all. I don't think there will be anything before tomorrow, so you go ahead. I have a couple of things I want to straighten out in my mind first."

He showed Robinson the way to the guest room, stopping for a moment in his own quarters to dig in a bottom drawer. From the drawer, he handed Robinson a Model 59 Smith and Wesson 9mm automatic.

Robinson took the weapon, jacked the slide back, picked up the ejected round, released the magazine, put the round back on top, slapped the magazine back in and reloaded the pistol.

Hendricks liked that. A man should always check his own weapons, no matter who says it is or is not loaded. The only way to be certain is to do it yourself.

From the dresser he took his old but familiar and comfortable Browning HP. Like him, it had been around and was still working. There were more modern versions, but this one he knew. He was comfortable with it. A creature of habit, he thought. Maybe I'm losing the capacity for change.

Returning to the living room, he sat in his favorite chair, by the fireplace. Laying the pistol on the end table by his right hand, he turned the butt so it would be in the right position if he should have to pick it up.

He didn't think about. It was just something you did. Here it was still wise to take normal precautions. His work here in the past had cost the terrorists much. It was never outside the realm of possibility that one day they might try to even up the score.

He sat long that night thinking. He thought about his men in Bokala and about the Colliers, the father and son. He liked them. He also thought about Washington, who should be getting settled into L.A. now, and if he could pull it off there. He hoped that Washington would be able to contact some of the names he had given him.

A rumble of thunder overhead gave a few seconds' warning before the first heavy drops of rain began to beat on the roof. The wind was picking up. The night would be cool. Most people didn't think it was cold in the tropics, but in the mountains it often got down into the forties.

He liked the rain. It helped one to think more clearly. It covered fears and doubts, made the thinking softer, easier.

He didn't know if they'd be able to pull this one off. There were so many things that could go wrong. And at this point, there was little he could do about it. The men he would get. And with the help of General Ponce, he had accessed the arms. It was a start.

He would have to communicate with Old Man Collier sometime tomorrow and give him a run-down on his progress. He would go ahead and make arrangements to purchase the medical supplies Ponce wanted. This he could do out of the deposits Anderson had made to his accounts in Belgium. There would be enough there to handle the arms and a bit more. That would be his contribution to the job.

The plan itself was strange enough, but it allowed latitude for change. The most important thing was to get into the country. Once they were there, if it didn't wash, changes could be made.

Right now getting into the country was mostly going to be up to Washington to do. Once in Bokala they might still have an ace to play: Kelo!

Kelo said he owed Hendricks. Why? What did that mean exactly? The man was obviously playing his own game. To what purpose? And to whose benefit?

Questions. The night was filled with questions and not many answers.

The coals in the fire were covered with gray ash, and a gray, misty dawn was just beginning to creep up the side of the mountains over the dark pines surrounding the house when Hendricks at last lay his body down, falling into an uneasy and troubled sleep. The Browning was on the night stand by his bed, the butt turned to fit his hand.

On the grounds outside the house, Tino walked in the shadows of the trees, staying out of the glow of the lights. Several times he saw the *jefe*'s shadow pass by the window as Hendricks walked the tiled floors. Tino wished he could help him, but even though he could not, he would see that no harm came to this house this night.

The Galil was cold and wet. The rain was good. It would keep him from getting too sleepy.

TEN

Redstar Productions and its studio head, Allison Chalmers, were only too pleased to welcome Mr. Jones with open arms and a Mercedes limo. Washington was met at LAX by Chalmers personally.

After Mr. Collier said that his son was to be executive producer on the project and would be coming into L.A. within the week to oversee things personally, Chalmers got his ass into high gear.

The Colliers were the bank, and without a bank, there were no movies. If there were no movies, then his dread that his career might end up with him as an attendant in a 24-hour quick market in Orange County might prove prophetic. He didn't know how to do anything else.

Chalmers didn't know what Mr. Jones's project was but he had never seen financing put together so fast. At Interstate Bank there was a letter of credit already established for eighteen million. There were larger budgets, but this was definitely respectable and worthy of attention.

When Washington checked into his room at the Hollywood Hilton, there was champagne, as well as a fruit basket from the studio, on the rosewood dining table. A card said that they were with the personal compliments of Mr. A. Chalmers.

Washington liked it. The rooms were spacious with thick plush pearl-gray carpeting, a separate kitchen and bedroom. It was more like a rich man's apartment, but at four hundred dollars a day it should have been.

Chalmers paid off the bellboy. Ten dollar tips were the norm, and on a good day a bell boy could take in several hundred dollars.

Sitting casually on the silk-covered sofa, Chalmers tried to look interested but not overly. He was a bit embarrassed that no one had told him what the project was.

"By the way, Mr. Jones, I've arranged limo service if you wish, and there is a Mercedes in your name in the hotel parking lot."

Washington smiled at him as he popped the top on the champagne. "Thank you, Mr. Chalmers. That is very considerate of you. I am sure we will get along famously."

Chalmers stood up to take the glass of wine offered him by Washington.

"I do hope so. I don't know how to tell you this . . . but I have no idea what your film is about. I haven't seen a treatment, much less a script."

Washington smiled gracefully at him as he sipped his wine, holding the crystal stem between two finger tips.

"Not to worry, Mr. Chalmers. The reason you have not seen anything is that there is nothing to see."

He stopped Chalmers's confused query with a movement of his champagne glass.

"Please don't concern yourself. This project is secret, very secret, and I want to keep it that way for some time. In fact, do not be surprised if I elect to use some people who are not from L.A. to do the job. I have my reasons, and Mr. Collier agrees with me. But—just for your ears and no others—I will give you a hint of what is to be."

Washington paused dramatically. He was enjoying himself tremendously. He thought he might even have a future in the films if he could fool this turkey.

"I'm all ears, Mr. Jones."

Washington choked back a laugh at the thought of a man who was all ears.

"Ahh, yes. Well,"—he lowered his voice to just above a whisper—"we are going to do a film on Bokala!"

He pronounced it with such authority that once more Chalmers was hesitant to ask, but he did.

"And just what is a Bokala, Mr. Jones?"

Washington refilled his glass and Chalmers's. "It is a country in Africa. One which has just recently gone through a revolution. During a fierce battle at the airfield, the new president, one Leopoldo Okediji, destroyed a mercenary force. A few escaped in one of the aircraft, but those on the ground were either killed or taken prisoner. It was not a small fight, Mr. Chalmers. It was a major battle, and the Africans won out over the white mercenaries.

"It was a historic moment in African history and a triumph against white oppression. What we are going to do is a film on the man, Leopoldo Okediji, and the defeat of the mercenaries at the airfield. It is today. It is timely. And it will be one hell of a film!"

Chalmers raised his glass. "Marvelous idea. Are you going to go on location with it?"

Washington nodded. "Of course. If it is possible,

and I think it will be. We will have the actual African soldiers who were at the original fight play their own parts in the film, perhaps even have a cameo spot by Okediji himself."

Chalmers sat back down on the sofa, a dreamy look in his eyes. "I did hear something about it, now that you mention it. Though, until now, I didn't realize the historic significance. But I can see it. White against black, and this time black wins. Africa for Africans. Fascists destroyed by the valor of the native peoples. Patriotism victorious over hired killers."

He sighed deeply once more. "Yes, yes, I can see it. This has nomination potential, Mr. Jones. I love it. Now, how can I help?"

Washington sat down beside him, leaning back against the smooth, cool silk. "First, keep this between us. Mr. Collier has put this in my hands because, if you know anything about me, I am without a doubt the best qualified to deal with it. I will need an office here for some time and a secretary. One who knows how to keep her mouth shut and avoid those who ask too many questions. I want you to put a couple of researchers on the job and come up with a rough story line."

Washington took an envelope out his inside breast pocket.

"This is a rundown on the chain of events that led to the battle. I think you will find it fascinating. Please be certain to find writers who have the same sensitivities that we do. I don't want any rednecks screwing around with this."

Chalmers understood perfectly. He put the envelope carefully into his own breast pocket, handling it in such a manner as to assure Jones that he would give it all the care and attention it deserved. This was to be a film with action and a message, true social relevance.

He wondered if he should ask Mr. Jones if he had thought about casting. Perhaps Poitier would be interested in the part of Okediji? Well, he would save that for later.

"Anything else you require?" Chalmers asked.

Washington stood up. "Yes. I want this done fast. I expect to have a treatment in my hands within ten working days and not one day later. Put as many people on it as you need, but make certain that they keep their mouths shut about the project. I don't want anything to leak until *we* are ready for it."

The *we* was intended to make Chalmers feel more a part of it. Washington moved close to Chalmers and put his hand on his shoulder. "One other thing, Allison, and this is not from me. It's from the old man. If word of this does leak out, Mr. Collier said for me to tell you to start looking for another line of work."

Suddenly Chalmers's vision of being behind the counter of an all-night market seemed dreadfully close.

Washington spoke sympathetically, saying, "Don't worry, Allison. We just have to keep the lid on this for a while longer, which is one reason why I will be using so many outsiders. They won't be in L.A., and they won't be starting rumors.

"The only people you will admit anything to will be those I tell you are okay. You know, such as the Bokalan ambassador if he calls to confirm my position with you. Things of that nature. Anyone else and we might have a lot of trouble.

"There are people, including some in political office, who would not want this project to come down. Think of yourself as an intelligence officer in a great struggle for right. Between us, we can do this. We are the front-line soldiers, and it is up to us to set the example."

Chalmers left feeling that he was on the front line of something significant. Jones was to do the actual work, but with his guidance and supervision, this film could be really important. He did not really like the idea that Jones was going outside the establishment to get his crew and cast, but it had been made very clear that Jones was to have his way. Chalmers was to assist him in every way, even if Jones's requests seemed a bit bizarre.

Washington wasted no time. He took out the short list of names Hendricks had given him. On it were some names of men, men Hendricks knew personally. All had been veterans at one time or another and now worked in Hollywood. Two were scriptwriters, the others worked as stunt men, and one, a man named Donald Milton, was a special effects expert.

Hendricks had been insistent about trying to get him. Milton had been in the Congo in 1954 with Six Commando. He would be able to help put together the rest of the film crew, and it really didn't matter if they belonged to the union. All they had to do was look as if they knew how to operate the equipment.

Washington grunted; it was not going to be easy. He needed about thirty men for the film crew, including grips, gaffers and lighting techs. He also had to keep them away from Chalmers as much as possible.

The first number he called was for George Hooker, returned Special Forces sergeant major, now a would-be scriptwriter and technical advisor who still did a little outside work. If Milton didn't know who to get, Hooker would. It was still a small club. Every major city in the world had its underground of ex and active soldiers of fortune or those who had served in regular armies and would be ready to go again.

Washington reached a recording machine, which asked for him to leave his name and number. He did so, but at the front of his message, he said into the mouthpiece, "This is about some business with Hendricks. Urgent. If you can, meet me tonight at nine in the restaurant of the Hollywood Hilton. Ask for Mr. Jones."

The next call was to Milton. He had better luck; he reached an office in the valley, where there were several movie special effects companies. A flat female voice, which reminded Washington of one of his drill instructors, answered his call with "Magic Milt Special Effects Company."

Washington identified himself, saying, "Good afternoon. I am Mr. Jones of New York, and I will be doing a film for Redstar. We have a very tight schedule, and if it would be possible, I would like to have a meeting with your Mr. Milton as soon as possible. This evening if it could be done."

The flat voice warmed up by half a degree when he mentioned Redstar. "I don't know about this evening, Mr. Jones."

Washington put on his smoothest sound. "My

dear, I assure you that this is a major production, and
time lost is money lost. Also, please inform Mr.
Milton as soon as possible that he was recommended to me by a mutual friend, a Mr. Martin
Hendricks. Please try to convince Mr. Milton to
contact me as soon as possible. It is urgent."

The secretary hung up after agreeing to do her
best. She liked the sound of "urgent" and "major
production." They could mean a contract that went
far beyond union scale.

"Who was that, Annie?" Milt looked up from his
workbench, where he was working on a remote wire
release device.

Annie Simpson was Milt's girl friend, bookkeeper,
partner and bodyguard. He stood when fully erect
about five feet and five compact, well conditioned
and muscled inches. Annie was closer to six feet
without shoes and over it with heels. She was not
plain but not pretty. What she was was strong.
Strong in body and in bed. She could whip most men
her size in a fair fight, and she didn't fight fair. Her
only real passion was Milt and things that were
important to him.

Leaving her desk, she moved over to him and ran
her fingers through his short-cropped curly brown
hair.

"I think we might have a live one, honey. That
was a producer named Jones. He said he's doing a
film for Redstar, big budget, and needs you urgently.
Oh yes, he also said that you were recommended to
him by someone named Martin Hendricks.

"Does that ring a bell? I don't know the name. Is it
someone from your mysterious past?" She teased
him. Then she noted the tensing between his shoul-

der blades as his body straightened up from the workbench.

"Hendricks, you said. Martin Hendricks?"

"That's what he said, honey."

Milton came up to his full height, and his face reset itself in a strange manner. Annie had seen that look before but only in some old pictures of him when he was in Vietnam. It frightened her.

"Call him back, set a meeting for tonight and put off any other business till I have had a chance to talk to him," he ordered—something he didn't do very often, but when he did, he meant it and she knew it.

Her voice and back stiffened, too. This had a bad feel to it, and she didn't know why. She called Jones back and confirmed a meeting for nine that evening in the hotel restaurant.

"Okay, honey, it's confirmed, this evening at nine. But who is this Hendricks and where did you know him? You never told me anything about him."

Milt's voice turned flatter than hers. "There was never any need for you to know, and there isn't any need now. So drop it."

She did. She knew there were times in his life that he never talked about. There were gaps of months and even years that were never mentioned. She didn't know where he had been or what he had been doing, and he never gave her the chance to try and pull it out of him.

He had made it very clear when they first started going together that if she wanted to stay with him, she had to accept the fact that some things in the past were best left alone.

ELEVEN

Washington was at his table a half hour early. He wanted a little time to think. He knew only that Milton had said he was coming. As for others, he had called the remaining three names. Two of the numbers were out of service, and on the last a voice informed him in no uncertain terms that he was out of the business and planned to stay that way, IOU to Hendricks or not! He was out. He hung up with a definite *no* click in the receiver.

Washington ordered a tall scotch and soda. He knew better than to drink heavily. From his recent experience with men like this, he knew he'd have to walk and talk carefully. They were sensitive, especially when they didn't know you. The only reason they would come was that Washington had used the name of Hendricks. That didn't necessarily mean they believed him. He would have to establish his credibility very rapidly.

"God," he thought, "this shit is moving fast. That old dude is heavy. When he says something is, then it is what he says it is. The sucker is bad time, heavy duty." It was hard for him to think that just days ago he had been in Bokala. Now he was a movie producer living in a four-hundred-dollar-a-day suite in Hollywood. His life had gone through some radical changes since Hendricks had had his ass hijacked for the Bokala job. He didn't know what the future days or weeks would bring. Whatever it was, it was going to be interesting.

His thoughts were interrupted by a shadow crossing over his table.

He looked up at a short, squarely built man with reddish hair and a face that only a tank could resemble.

"Jones, I'm Hooker." That was it. The voice wasn't friendly or hostile; it was matter-of-fact. Washington knew from Hendricks something about Hooker's past. He retired as sergeant major from Special Forces, but while in Nam, he'd received a battlefield commission and the rank of captain. Then, after the war he was riffed back to sergeant major. He'd done jobs for anti-Castro elements, been in Africa during the Biafra cluster fuck and a number of other situations.

He looked it. His face had a strange nose that had been broken more than once and was as square as his body. The only small thing on him was his legs. They looked too small to support the weight of the massive upper body. Very pale washed-out blue eyes looked down at Washington, analyzing, weighing and judging. Washington had the feeling that he would have to walk very softly around this one; the dude was bad. He'd hurt you.

Washington stood up. This man deserved that courtesy. Even if you didn't know anything about his past, a smart man would be polite. Washington's mama always told him being polite don't hurt none, with this man anything else could.

"Please, Mr. Hooker, won't you sit down?"

Hooker did so. Washington eased himself slowly back into his seat, not knowing why he was moving so slowly. "Mr. Hooker, I do appreciate you coming over like this on such short notice. But it is important. I also know that you will have to be convinced of my bona fides first."

Hooker said nothing to that but ordered a mineral water and lime when the waiter passed by.

Uneasy, Washington continued. "The boss needs you and some of your friends for a special job."

Hooker broke in. "Where is he now?"

"He should be in Guatemala."

"Do you know his home number?"

"Yes."

"What is it?"

Washington hesitated a moment, then he knew why Hooker wanted the number. Hooker already knew it. "Certainly. 303 402 San Lucas."

Hooker relaxed a bit but not all the way. "Okay, you got that part right. But you could have got the number from another source. How do I know that you didn't?"

Washington took a long sip of his scotch and soda and wished that he'd ordered a mineral water.

"Why don't you call him yourself? You can do it from the lobby and bill it to my room. He's expecting a call from me sometime tonight. If you want to make it, it's all right with me. I'll wait here. But if you can get through—you know how the lines are in that part of the world—don't hang up. I need to talk to him, too."

Hooker stood up. "Good idea. I'll do that very thing, right now. Then we'll know if we have anything else to talk about, Mr. Jones."

Hooker left for the lobby, and Washington felt a sense of relief wash over him. This son of a bitch had the same feel to him that Duke did, only without the sense of humor.

He was just getting settled back down when he saw another man enter the restaurant and look around the tables. The head waiter spoke to him a moment, then pointed out Washington at his table.

Milton weaved his way through the evening diners.

His manner was a bit easier than that of Hooker, but it was still wary.

"You Jones?"

"Yes, I am."

Milton pointed to the glass of mineral water on the opposite side of the table. "Who else is here?"

Washington looked at the glass. "Someone I think you know, George Hooker. He's on the phone now trying to reach Hendricks in Guatemala."

Milton sat down between Hooker's place and Washington. "The Hook's checking you out, huh?"

Washington smiled. "Yes, he's doing exactly that."

Milton lit up a Winston, took a drag and said, "I did some checking, too. Redstar verifies that you are a new hot shot from the East Coast come in to do a major film. They won't say what the film is about. But they did say you have the budget and are for real. Are you for real, Jones?"

Washington smiled broadly for the first time since he had come into L.A.

"Not by a long shot, Mr. Milton. I am the phoniest son of a bitch in Hollywood."

That didn't seem to bother Milton at all. He

leaned back in the chair, relaxing. "I don't know about that. There are a lot of people here who qualify for that honor. But if you're not a producer, what the hell are you, and what do you want from me?"

"Let's wait a few minutes before I explain anything. When Hooker comes back and if he's satisfied, then we'll have something to talk about. I think you'll feel better if he verifies my story. The real story."

Milton ordered a Bud Light while they were waiting and talked show business to Washington, giving him the story of his life, which he usually found fascinating, more so than his listeners. He wasn't shy, because even if Washington was bogus he had to know a good part of his history or he wouldn't have been there. So he wasn't really telling him anything critical.

He had gotten into the business after the service. He'd been a demo man. His father had been a prop man for thirty years and got him into the movies. He liked it. He got to play with things that went bang in the night, or day, and spent most of his free time developing new gags for stunt men or ways to blow things or people up without killing them. He'd met Hendricks in Africa. He still took some outside work every now and then, to break the routine and because he liked it.

He was just getting to the part of his life where he'd met Annie when Hooker came back in. Hooker gave Milton an honest smile when he saw him, and Washington relaxed even more. Milton got up, and he and Hooker embraced each other, then kissed on the mouth.

The only other time Washington had seen this happen was the night before they took off from Bir Misaha for Bokala, when the mercenaries had their party, if that was the right word for it. When the drinking was done, each man had turned to embrace and kiss the man nearest him. It was not sexual; it was a way of being part of a brotherhood and of saying good-bye or in some cases, such as now, of greeting someone else who had lived on the edge.

Milton sat back down, ignoring Washington. He asked Hooker, "Did you reach the boss?"

Hooker got back into his chair, his manner much more relaxed. Taking a sip of mineral water, he cleared his throat before saying, "Yeah. He was home. He didn't say much over the phone. You know the spooks can tap into everything coming in from overseas. All he did say was to talk to the man and to listen to him serious. I told him you wanted to speak to him, but he was on his way out. He said he'd call you in your room later tonight."

He turned from Milton, locking those pale eyes on Washington. "All right, Mr. Jones or whoever you are, we are ready to listen serious."

Washington cleared his throat, coughing slightly. "Good. Because what I am going to tell you, you ain't going to believe. But we have gone over it and think it can be pulled off.

"So for the next few minutes, please just listen. After I'm finished, I'll answer any questions you have, if I can. Hendricks said to give it all to you, the good and the bad. And there is plenty of bad."

They ordered dinner but didn't taste it. Washington told them everything. The raid on the palace, the battle at the airfield, the escape, Hendricks now going back in.

Hooker asked, "How are you going to get back in? I've been in that part of the world, and the people there are paranoid normally. After your raid there and the escape, I'd think that Okediji would be very touchy about anyone, blacks included, coming in and asking questions about his prisoners."

Washington agreed with him. "You're right. That's why I'm here. We're doing the stage setting now. My next move is to return to Bokala and to meet with Okediji. You say you've been in that part of the world, but I was born there. I'm going in with credentials that can be verified. I am a real producer with a real company and have a multi-million-dollar budget to do the story of Okediji's victory over the foreign mercenaries who invaded his land and were destroyed at Bokala International Airport. I'm going to make him a star."

Milton broke in; he was beginning to get excited. He saw where Washington was going.

"Right. If you can go in like that, you'll have every reason to ask about the prisoners and do the recon. One thing I've learned here over the years is that everyone, but everyone, in the world dreams one time or another of being a movie star.

"If this Okediji asshole buys it and you can suck him in, he'll open the doors for you and fall over himself doing it."

"Right," acknowledged Washington. "That's the key—his ego. We have another card to play there, which I have to check out. If this goes right, we will have a man on Okediji's staff on our side. He opened the door for the rescue of the hostages held by Mehendi. Hendricks thinks this man's playing his own game. We don't know what it is, but it doesn't matter. If we can get him to go with us on this, he might be able to open the doors again."

Hooker pushed his coffee cup aside and lit up a smoke. "Then what you want us to do is make up part of the contingency plan. If things shake down right, you'll want us to locate enough men with combat experience to make up a film crew."

Washington nodded.

Milton and Hooker looked at each other and grinned.

"No problem. L.A. is full of strange people, including a surprising number like us. I think we can give you most if not all of the men you need in two weeks," Hooker said.

They were in. It was a start.

"All right," said Washington. "Now, we are funded on this one for section leaders, which you and Milton will be. The job pays twenty-five thousand. For the other shooters, twenty each. We are in luck with this. We have Daddy Warbucks on our side. A million or two don't mean shit to him. I told you about his son being there and how his girl friend was killed. The kid wants payback, and the old man is a real old fashioned hardnose.

"We have just about an open checkbook for this one, and he says spend it if it gets the job done. If it doesn't, he said for us to find a hole to hide in and pull it in on top of us."

Hooker and Magic Milt were in without having to say so. Everyone knew it. Milton asked Washington,

"Okay, but now how do we put it together and keep it quiet?"

Washington ordered another drink for everyone. For himself, this time he ordered a mineral water and lime. Hooker, just to be contrary, ordered a scotch and water.

"All right," began Washington. "This is the way we think it should play. If you have any better suggestions, please let me hear them and I'll pass them on. A lot of this we're doing by ear. Okay, you contact your people and put them on standby for a tentative kick off date of June first. That gives us eight weeks.

"You don't give them any information other than that it will be a short-time job on site, but they will have to be on line for probably two weeks. The job itself will go down in one day."

He followed the same basic formula Hendricks had. "Tell them it is risky, but that's what they're paid for. Don't tell anyone who the others on the team will be. Once we have a movement date, they'll be brought together. At that point, no one goes back home till the job is over, one way or another."

"Look, some of these guys are a bit hard-nosed about what they get into. What if they give us a ration of shit when they hear about the job and they don't want to go?" Hooker asked.

"That is going to be part of your job, to make sure we don't have that problem. Tell them it's tough on the front. If they sign on, there's five thousand immediate payment. The balance on completion. Once we've got them all together, it'll be hard for anyone to back out without seeming to be a coward. Peer pressure should keep them in. If it doesn't, then

I know that Hendricks will have something in mind to keep them out of the way till the job is over. Maybe he'll drop them on a desert island or something for a few weeks. I don't know. All I am doing is passing on what he told me to say."

TWELVE

It was after midnight before Hendricks was able to get through on the phone to Washington. As was the case all too often, the phone lines in Guate were screwed up. It was a great country, but there were still some things which seemed to operate on a system that should have been replaced decades earlier. But that was the third world.

His talk with Washington was short and guarded. All he could tell Washington at this point was that he had located the merchandise they would need and for him to keep playing his game and to start making his arrangements to return to Bokala.

The night was long and, for one of the few times in his life, lonely. He missed the familiar presence of Claude in the house. He made the long hours shorter. It had almost become a ritual with them. The midnight watch, as they planned and talked over an operation. Now he was gone. Him and Duke, the cunt junkie. If he didn't get Duke out, the sound of hearts breaking from Nashville to Honduras would make the people in Guatemala think another earthquake was happening.

When Robbie got up the following morning, Hendricks was already at work. It was six in the morning. He just caught the tail end of a conversation Hendricks was having over the phone.

"I know, Dutch. But I'm going to make it right. You know that. I would never leave anyone behind. That's why I'm calling."

Pause.

"I understand, but ask them anyway. There will be some, and they know the layout. If they'll go back, I want them."

Robbie saw a look of minor consternation pass over Hendricks's face.

"All right. Look for him on Wednesday or Thursday."

Pause.

"Yes. Yes. I know!"

Pause.

"Lebe wohl."

He hung up the receiver, picked up his cup of coffee, which had gone cold, tasted it, made a face and set it back down.

"Good morning."

"Good morning."

Hendricks leaned back in his chair and raised his arms over his head to stretch out muscles gone stiff from too many hours of sitting. He groaned a bit, then ran his hands over his face as if the action could give him a few more minutes of awareness before the need for sleep pushed him down.

"Robbie, are you ready to do some traveling?"

"Sure, where to?"

"Europe. I want you to go and meet the Dutchman. He is a little upset over the way his last contract with me turned out. He's a tightfisted, tough old bastard, but he does worry a bit. What I want you to do is get the rest of our people through him. We need fifty. Once they come in, it will be up to you to handle the interviews. The Dutchman will inform everyone beforehand that, as always, if they are accepted they must be ready to travel immediately with no good-byes or last farewells.

"Once you have accepted a man, he is yours. The Dutchman will arrange a safe house for you and them. Tell them nothing, other than that it will be a short-term job. Once you have them, keep them out of sight and tell them not to cut their hair. We'll want them as happy and unmilitary-looking as possible for the time being."

Robbie yawned a bit, stretched out his own arms, arched his back, and was pleased at the cracking sound that came from his vertebrae as they snapped.

"Okay, but what was that 'if they'll go' stuff? It sounds like you're trying to get back on line some of those who got out on the first plane."

Hendricks got up, moving around his desk to look at the *National Geographic* map of the world on his wall. His eyes were on the region of central Africa.

"That's right. If I can get them back, it will save a lot of time, and give me some people who have been on the ground and know it. They will also be able to help a lot with the new men."

Hendricks left his office, going into the living room. He turned off the outside lights around the house. That was the signal that let Tino know that those inside were up and moving. Only then did Tino go to his own quarters, a small whitewashed block house at the base of the property, and look for his own missing sleep. The *jefe* was up and awake. Now he could rest.

Hendricks left Robbie to his own devices. There would be nothing they could do for the next three hours, until things opened up in the city. Till then, Hendricks would sleep.

Robbie was just getting ready to fix his own breakfast when a tap at the door brought his head around. A smiling, dark face with two front teeth missing was looking in the window at him. Alejandra, Tino's wife and Hendricks's housekeeper, was grinning at him shyly. Placing his pistol back in his rear pocket, he opened the door. Alejandra said to him politely, *"Buenas dias, señor permite mi."* She stooped down to take up a wicker basket at her feet, filled with food from the market at San Lucas. She set it gracefully on her head and came inside. She saw that Robbie had been in the kitchen. Shyly, she pointed at the stove and asked, *"Desayuno?"*

Robbie didn't speak much Spanish, but the meaning was clear.

He nodded his head, saying, "Sí, sí, por favor."

Alejandra set her basket down and waddled her stout figure happily into the kitchen, where she set about preparing food for the *jefe*'s guest. It was good to be doing something for the *jefe* again. He had been gone a long time. The house had been desolate in his absence.

She was used to strangers being in the house. In the years she had worked for Hendricks, she had seen many different people come and go. None, except for Duke and Becaude, seemed to stay very long. Though there had been a few times when they had had guests for a week or two. What they did or were going to do, she never asked and never thought to ask. It was not her concern.

What Hendricks did was all right with her. For had he not, when her daughter Orpha had nearly cut her finger off, taken them to a private hospital where he paid for everything, including something called a tendon resection? Her three-year-old daughter's finger would always be a bit shorter and fatter than the others. But it was a finger and not a stump, as so many children of the *campesinos* and poor had.

Her interest was in seeing that the inside of the house was taken care of. That included everything in it, even people. Somehow she had the vague idea that if someone was in the house, they were property of the *jefe's*. They were therefore to be maintained as well as the furniture.

She moved quietly, almost on tiptoe, so as not to disturb Hendricks in his room at the rear of the house. Robbie liked her being there, too. It had been a long time since he had been where a woman took care of things.

His wife had left him six years before. Too many overseas assignments. She needed a white picket fence that would be in the same place every day and neighbors who always spoke the same language. An old story. It might have been different if they'd had children, but then who could tell?

For the first time, he was able to take a good look around the house, which was more like a hunting lodge than a residence. But it suited a male existence. It had high beamed ceilings, a large fireplace and a small kitchen. The office had a low shelf of books, not many, but enough to tell one quite a bit about the man who lived here. Von Clausewitz and Sun Tzu; a number of books on weapons of the world, demolitions and explosives; several good volumes of history and archaeology; and a few classics, *I, Claudius* and Wells's *The Outline of History*, along with works by Descartes and Bacon.

On the living room wall, to the sides of the fireplace, were a few antique weapons, a couple of sabers from when Guatemala had a cavalry, muzzle-loading muskets, a court épée and a wide-bladed, sixteenth century–style sword. It all looked original. There was something about weapons which had been used that set them apart from copies. Copies of weapons never seemed as if they had been alive. These did. Someone real had worn and used them.

Of art works there were none. A few prints of bullfighters and some watercolors of the Indians of Guate in daily life, scenes that Robbie thought had probably come with the house when Hendricks took it over.

He picked up the copy of Sun Tzu, *The Art of War*, and thumbed through it. Like his own copy, it had been well used and, he was certain, well read. Robbie carried the book back into the kitchen to read while eating breakfast. He was still absorbed in the book, written before Christ, when he heard Hendricks stirring in his bedroom and the flash heater for the hot water in the kitchen come on.

In ten minutes, Hendricks was out of the bathroom and dressed in faded jeans and a long-sleeve khaki shirt, rolled up to his forearms. His eyes were clearer, and the set of his jaw was firm. The few hours' sleep had recharged and refreshed him.

Robbie knew from personal experience how soldiers and pilots adapted to getting by for days or even weeks on two or three hours of sleep a day.

Alejandra had a steaming mug of good, rich Guatemalan coffee ready for Hendricks as he came into the kitchen.

The phone rang just as he was putting his lips to the cup. He set the cup down on the dining room table, went over and picked up the receiver.

"Dige me."

Robbie heard him talk in Spanish for a few moments. From what little he could pick up, he knew that it was Tono saying something about General Ponce.

When Hendricks had hung up, he went back to his coffee, putting his nose over the edge of the cup to inhale the aroma.

"There's no coffee in the world like what they grow here. Even the instant stuff they sell here is three times better than anything you can buy in the States."

Robbie agreed. The coffee was exceptional. "Yeah, but now what do we do? Do you want me to make my reservations?"

Hendricks shook his head. "Not now. We'll go into town. I have a friend at one of the agencies; she'll take care of you. And we need to see General Ponce again. Tono says he has his shopping list of medical supplies ready."

He saw the clean plate on the table and smiled at Robbie.

"I see Alejandra's been taking care you."

Robbie nodded. "Better than home."

"Good. Now, if you're ready, let's move out. There's lots to do."

• • •

Tino was ready. Somehow he knew when the *jefe* would be up and moving. He'd opened the garage doors where the red Suzuki Samurai sat waiting for them. The *jefe* normally used it for running back and forth. When it was something more, there was a Land Cruiser or a late-model Buick with air conditioning, for trips to the South Coast or Puerto Barrios.

The day was clear. It wouldn't rain again until the sun began to set. For now, it was crystal crisp and green. Just before Mixco, there was an overview from which one could see Guatemala City spread out in the valley below. The population was two million and growing. If they didn't do something about the birthrate, by the turn of the century there would be over six million.

Taking the same route in reverse, they turned onto Fifth Avenida and Eleventh Calle and headed for the parking tower across from the Quijote. Hendricks left the Samurai there with the attendant and took Robbie up the stairs where there was a small row of shops, including a travel agency, a photographer's studio and a jewelry store.

Taking Robbie inside the travel agency, he turned him over to Isabel, a long-haired, hazel-eyed beauty who could have been on the cover of *Vogue*.

Robbie explained to Isabel what he wanted and gave her his passport. She looked at him with openly interested eyes, saying he would need a visa for France, but she could take care of it. The agency would send a messenger over to the French Consulate with his passport and have it and the visa back before lunch.

Robbie thought he might be falling in love. She smiled at him with dazzling teeth and said she would bring the itinerary and his documents over to Don Quijote's when it was all put together.

THIRTEEN

Hendricks left Robbie at the Quijote while he returned to the cuartel general for his meet with Ponce. He was gone an hour and a half. By the time he returned, Robbie and Isabel were having lunch together.

"Everything in order?"

Robbie shook his head up and down as he chewed on a forkload of river shrimp baked in butter and garlic. Swallowing the mouthful, he pushed it all the way down with swig of Gallo Beer. "Right. She's got it all lined up. I fly out on Iberia tomorrow morning, direct to Spain, from there to Brussels."

Hendricks ordered whiskey and soda from Carlos, who had appeared magically at his elbow. Hendricks smiled with affection at the small ex-pug as he left to fill the order and returned in less than thirty seconds, setting the glass in front of Hendricks with a flourish of the wrist, which would have done service to a magnum of Dom Perigon.

Isabel finished her shrimp, looked at the two men and knew that at that moment she was excess. Leaning over, she whispered in Robbie's ear, winked at Hendricks and excused herself, returning to her office.

Both Robbie and Hendricks watched in admiration the swish of her hips as she strode out. Strode was the operative word. She moved with sure determination and timing, and every muscle in her buttocks was firmly rotating in carefully synchronized movement.

Robbie sighed deeply, letting his air out slowly as if savoring it. "I think I'm in love."

Smiling with understanding, Hendricks said, "I know. But be careful. They'll kill you with love or a machete. The Latin ladies are a bit jealous about their men, and they'll decide when you are their man, not you. But you could do much worse."

Robbie grunted a bit sourly. "I already have."

Hendricks looked around him at the lunch crowd, which was just beginning to come in. Spaniards were predominate, but there was a mixture of Germans, Swiss, American kids with the Peace Corps, and Chapinas, as the Guatemalans called themselves.

Dario was busy socializing with Paco, a lean hawk-faced Spanish coffee planter from the Alta Ver Paz. He saw Hendrick's eye wandering around and nodded at him, then returned to his conversation.

The stereo played classical Spanish music, the kind that sounded as if someone had his nuts caught in a vise—high-pitched, whining, with a very strong Arab influence, a legacy from the time when the Moors were the masters of most of Spain. The Spanish customers loved it. Hendricks could tolerate the sound but thought that you probably had to grow up with it to appreciate it.

Forcing his eyes back into his sockets after Isabel had left, Robbie asked Hendricks, "Things go okay with the man?"

"Yes. I got his shopping list. I'll send it over to
Collier by DHL this afternoon. He can put someone
on it. Right now, you just get on over to Belgium and
get the Dutchman moving. I stopped by my bank on
the way and made arrangements for a wire transfer
to be waiting for you when you reach Brussels.
Spend what you need, but don't waste any of it. This
money was my retirement plan."

At this time of the day most businesses in Latin
America came if not to a complete stop, then to a
definite slowdown. Lunchtime was a tradition, and
depending on the business, it lasted for two to three
hours. During this time, Hendricks usually enjoyed
himself by watching the customers come and go.

Some of them also watched him, not all of them
with friendly eyes. There was a section of the
population, both foreign and domestic, who didn't
like the man with the military look. He was no
secret. Many knew or felt they knew what his line of
work was. Not all approved.

The Guatemalans were usually much more tolerant than the foreigners, especially the young Germans, who were still whipping themselves with
guilt complexes over the Nazi era. Hendricks wondered if it was possible that an excess of social
responsibility was making their faces break out but
figured it was just adolescence.

His meeting with Ponce had gone very well. He
didn't mention or ask about the recent demise of the
smugglers. That would have been in bad taste. And
to be sure, their dying meant nothing to him. They
had just gone a bit sooner than if they had been
taken into a military court. The moment the smug-

glers fired on the Guatemalan naval ship, they had signed their own death warrant.

Ponce, as always, was a perfect host. Coffee was brought in by his aide. They talked over small things for a few minutes before getting down to the business at hand. Hendricks gave him a list of the items he wanted. Ponce glanced at it casually and nodded his head.

Between them they had trust, trust proven over time. If Hendricks said he would get the medical supplies Ponce wanted, then that was that.

Ponce was even now having the arms repacked and crated for transport to Puerto Barrios. They would be stored in the warehouse of the army detachment stationed there, ready for the moment when Hendricks needed them.

Hendricks felt good about Ponce and the weapons, but he was still worried. There was no reason to feel bad about the way things had developed in the last few days; it was going fast, very fast. But would it be fast enough? He was afraid that each moment lost might cost the life of one of his men. And there was so much yet to do.

While Robbie was in Europe, he would have to return to the States for another meeting with the Colliers. That was the best bit of luck he'd had, Anthony and his father. Without them, he had no idea of what he would have done. With them, doors which should have been closed were easy to open. Wealth had the keys, keys to so many things. It could buy lives or take them, make presidents and senators, purchase arms or real estate.

He would take the morning flight out to Miami on Aviateca, then to New York. He didn't like the idea of using the phone any more than he had to. It was probably reasonably safe now, but as things progressed, it was going to be harder to keep everything under the hat. If the Americans or anyone else got suspicious, the phone would be his weakest link.

Therefore, when possible, he would have to handle meetings in person. He'd go to New York, then probably out to L.A. to tie up loose ends for Washington. Hooker and Milton would only go so far on Washington's word. They would want to meet with him before they got in too deep. He didn't blame them. This was not going to be a normal job, if there was such a thing in this line of work.

A rush of weariness came over him. He closed his eyes for a moment, blacking out the sounds of people dining. He had no appetite. So much to do. How many were left alive now. How many would there be if he got them out—No!—when he got them out. No time for negative thoughts. He would get them out or he would die there with them. That was his commitment. He didn't know if Robbie understood that. There was a time to die. It came to all. To some more than once. Robbie was a good man, but he'd been conventional for a very long time. For him, this was a break in all the years of routine. An adventure. Nothing wrong with that but he didn't have the motivation that Hendricks had. He didn't want Robbie to die thinking he was on some romantic quest.

Opening his eyes he saw a pen and ink caricature of Don Quijote over the bar—the thin, haggard face, bulbous eyes, scraggly beard—off to joust against windmills.

What they were going against were not windmills.

What they would face could and would kill without hesitation. Windmills . . . Perhaps, as with Quijote, it was better to be mad, then everything you did was clear and justifiable. Was it justifiable that he was going to take in another team and perhaps have them killed or taken captive? It could all go down the tube so very easily.

Dario had left his talk with Paco to answer the phone. It was a call for Hendricks. Dario screened all of Hendricks's calls personally.

He sent Carlos over to the table. Carlos whispered in Hendricks's ear, bringing him back to the present.

"*Gracias*, Carlos."

Getting up, he moved over to the bar, where the mad face of Don Quijote smirked at him with a knowing lunatic's nonsmile.

"Hendricks here," he said into the piece.

There was a pause, as he listened to the voice on the other end, and then a smile. Robbie knew he was talking to a friend. The conversation was short, ending with Hendricks saying, "Right, see you tonight at the house."

Coming back to the table, he said to Robbie, "We got company tonight. An old friend. I think you'll enjoy meeting him."

Robbie asked him. "Is he anyone who can help?"

Shaking his head from side to side, Hendricks answered, "No. He would if he could. He did last time. But for this I think it's best to keep him out of it.

"So don't let anything slip about what we have planned. He's sharp. He can read things out of your garbage that tell more about your life than your psychiatrist could learn in five years of therapy.

"He reads people. So don't let it worry you if he

talks like he knows everything. He may not know what we're doing, but he'll feel something. Just don't give him anything other than the time of day, and be careful with that."

It was near eight when a honk at the gate brought Tino up to open it for Vic Broadman. Hendricks went outside to greet him. Robbie was inside packing again. His clothes had been freshly ironed by Alejandra, even his shorts. He couldn't remember the last time he'd seen ironed shorts and T-shirts.

He heard Hendricks talking in the living room. When he got there, Vic was seated on the sofa. He gave Robbie an inquiring look. Hendricks was right. He could feel Broadman's mind going over him, analyzing, taking in everything and cataloging it. He felt that Broadman already had half of his life story figured out before Hendricks introduced them to each other.

When Vic stood up, Robbie saw that he moved a bit stiffly on his legs. He didn't ask. If Broadman wanted to tell him he would. Robbie poured drinks for all, and they sat down. The fire was going good, taking off some of the evening chill.

"Okay, Martin." He looked at Robinson, too, when he spoke. "What came down over there? I heard it was and wasn't a mess."

Hendricks sipped a thin scotch and water. "I guess that depends on which side of the fence you're on. We got the hostages out, as you know. But I had to leave a lot of my people behind. But you already know that."

Vic nodded. "Yeah, I heard." Vic heard many things. As political liaison officer at the embassy he was wired into a lot of input from D.C.

"I made it a point to hear, Martin. But what now? Are you going back in for them?"

Hendricks shook his head in a noncommittal manner.

"Vic, you know that whatever I say, you're going to believe what you want. If I say yes, you'll have to sit on the fence again. If I say no, you're not going to believe me. So let's just leave it at that. It'll be better for everyone."

Vic knocked back his drink. Then he said, "If that's how you want it, that's how it'll be. I just wanted to know if I could help you or not."

"I appreciate it, Vic, I really do. But at this time, there is nothing that you can do. But I won't forget it."

Vic changed his target to Robbie. "And you, Colonel, how did you get involved with this bandit? You know if you hang around him too long you're probably not going to live to a ripe old age."

Robbie picked his words, remembering what Hendricks had told him about Broadman. "I'll just have to take what comes. But for now, I'm content with things."

Vic laughed. "Martin told you to tighten up around me, didn't he? No, don't answer. I don't want to embarrass anyone. I know how he works. We've known each other since the old days in Africa. We weren't exactly on the same side, but that was politics, nothing personal."

Vic stood up, walking stiff-legged to the door. "Come on and walk me out, Martin." Turning back to Robbie, he said, "Be careful out there. It can get very lonesome sometimes. I can't help but think you might have had a brighter future if you had stayed in the service. But that's your choice. Good-bye, good luck."

Robbie gave him an offhand salute as he went out the door.

Tino was standing in the shadows near the fountain. When they came out, he moved back up to the gate to open it for Vic's car.

It was difficult for Vic to get up the small flight of steps to the parking area. But he wouldn't have let anyone help him, and Hendricks didn't ask.

When they reached the car and Vic was sure they were alone, he said, "Don't make any more calls to L.A. or Belgium. In fact, don't make a call to do anything more than order firewood. If it wasn't that you've got yourself connected with the Colliers, the hammer would probably have already fallen on you. Be careful, my friend, and come back safe."

They shook hands, and Hendricks watched as Vic's car pulled out of the driveway and back on the road to the city and the embassy. He wondered if he'd see him again.

When Hendricks came back inside Robinson said, "He's a sharp man, and I think he really would like to help. Why don't you use him?"

Hendricks shook his head in a negative. "No. I don't like putting Vic on the fence. He's American government, and I don't want him to compromise himself too much. He will help in his way; in fact, he already has. He knows what it's like on the edge. He's been there. He lost his leg in Vietnam."

Robinson didn't say anything, but he felt pleased that when he had seen Broadman he had had the feeling that he'd been there.

Checking his watch, he said, "Well, I guess that

wraps it for me. I'm going to put the body down. I have an early flight tomorrow. How about you?"

Hendricks nodded in agreement. "Go ahead. I'll be pulling out, too, but I'm going up to Tapachula, Mexico instead of flying directly to Miami. It's about a four-and-a-half hour drive. I'll take a flight out of there to Mexico City, then to Miami and on to New York and L.A.

"From what Vic said, they're keeping an eye on us here. It's too late to change your plans. If they've already got you located, they know where you're going. Changing flights or routes wouldn't matter much; they'd just pick you up on the other end when you cleared customs.

"So go ahead, just be careful and watch for tails. When you get settled, use a public phone for all your calls and let the Dutchman come for you. He'll know how to shake anyone who might be on you."

FOURTEEN

At five in the morning, Hendricks and Robbie left the house. Tino drove Robbie to Aurora Airport and let him off there to catch his flight to Spain. Then he headed the jeep for the coastal road, dropping off the plateau valley of Guatemala City and heading down five thousand feet to Esquintla. There they came onto the coastal road, and the climate changed dramatically from mountain chill to tropical heat, with banana palms and coconut orchards. At Esquintla, they turned north, passing through Mazatenango. Hendricks had gone crocodile hunting near there last year. They gassed up before going on past Retalhuleo and a grove of rubber trees.

Tino let Hendricks off at Tecun Uman, where he cleared immigration and passed on over the bridge to the Mexican side of the border. The Samurai was in Hendricks's name, and it would have been a hassle for him to make out the documents permitting Tino to cross into Mexico and return to Guatemala with it.

On the Mexican side, Hendricks caught a taxi to the airport at Tapachula. Through one of the money changers who hung in clusters around both sides of the border, he changed only enough dollars to cover the cab fare.

135

His flight from Tapachula stopped at Oaxaca, then went directly to Mexico City, where he changed planes for a flight to Miami, then on to New York. It was the long, roundabout way, and he did not arrive until 0600 the morning after he was originally scheduled to set down at Kennedy. Then it was almost another hour in a taxi to the old Warwick Hotel on Sixth Avenue.

Once he'd checked in, he crashed for three hours before calling Collier's offices.

Jameson sent a chauffeured Mercedes stretch limousine to bring him to the building near Central Park. He was at the door to greet Hendricks personally and escort him up to the executive offices of Collier Enterprises.

Hendricks was ushered past secretaries, accountants and salesmen of every ilk, until they reached the inner sanctum of Anthony Collier II. Jameson nodded at the professionally attractive, fortyish secretary, who still had most of her too-sharp, tailored New York looks, and they were permitted to enter Collier's office. The secretary had given Hendricks a look that he had seen on the faces of animals who were about to feed on fresh killed meat. He was glad to get away from there. Predatory women always made him nervous.

He was surprised. From the expensive layout outside and the number of people employed, he'd expected one of those Hollywood set offices where everything was color coordinated, stainless steel and modern paintings. Instead he found an office that could have belonged to any small town real estate broker. One plain old oak desk, two chairs, a small sofa, over which hung a calendar from Collier's mechanic years. The desk could have been bought at a Goodwill sale. The only impressive thing in the office was Collier. His clothes cost more than all the furnishings put together.

Hendricks could see that Collier was pleased at his reaction.

Getting up, Collier came around his cheap desk to shake hands. "Gets them every time," Collier said. "Some sharpie will come in ready to hustle me for millions on some good deal or another. This really throws them off. And to tell the truth, this is pretty much the same kind of shit I had when I got started. It serves to remind me. Keeps me on my toes so to speak."

He pulled out one of the chairs for Hendricks and told Jameson to bring coffee. When Jameson had left, Collier said, "Well! How's it going on your end? Your package just reached me at nine this morning. I've barely had a chance to look at it. But I see no problems in acquiring what you need, though it seems somewhat excessive. But never mind, if that's what you think you want, you shall have it. But, I expected to hear from you before now. I've talked with our new Mr. Jones several times and, of course, the president of the studio. Both assure me all is progressing well."

Hendricks rubbed the back of his neck. He was still stiff from the flight. "I would have called but my phones are probably tapped. A friend of mine who's in a position to know advised me not to use them anymore. I listen to such advice very seriously. At any rate, I'm here now. Before I go any further, I want to know if you and your son are still committed."

Jameson came in with the coffee, poured two cups

and looked at Collier to see if he should stay. A slight incline of the head toward the door and Jameson was gone.

"Yes, we're still in. I told you that at the beginning. Jones is well established on the coast. His cover is perfect. Everyone out there thinks he is a hotshot doing a special production. But how about you? Are you making any progress?"

Hendricks sipped the coffee and tried not to make a face. He had become too accustomed to the rich brew from the highlands of Guate.

"Yes. By the way, the medical supplies on that list are in exchange for arms and accessories we need. They should be on their way to Puerto Barrios on the Caribbean coast by now. I'll arrange for a payment of one hundred thousand dollars to be made to any account you specify to cover the cost of General Ponce's shopping list."

Collier shook his impressive gray-haired bulldog head from side to side. "Don't worry about it. I can cover it."

Hendricks stood up, hoping his knees wouldn't crack from the hours of sitting on planes. "No, Mr. Collier! This a matter in which I have to do what I can, and that includes what money I have. This is not a matter of profit for me. This, as it is for Anthony—though in a somewhat different way—is something personal that has no price."

Collier liked that. It was always a better and more secure deal when the people involved were also at risk with their money. Hendricks was risking not only his money but also his life. Collier had done deals with far less security than that.

"Are you able to get all the men you need?" he asked.

"I think we'll pull it together. I'll know more once I get to the coast and talk with Washington and some of my friends there. But I think it can be handled. Right now, Robinson is in Europe. I'll probably talk to him sometime tomorrow. By then he'll have had a chance to get a feel for things. What we need right now is to arrange transport for the weapons out of Guatemala. Probably the best bet would be to transfer them to the duty-free zone on Grand Turk Island. Once we have the team and aircraft together, all we have to do is make a stop-over there, pick up the cargo and keep on moving. I can have friends in Guate arrange the necessary documents, so the customs people don't get too nosy about what's in the crates."

He thought of Antonio. The man was gifted when it came to fine "negotiations" of this nature.

Collier nodded. "Good, it sounds as if things are starting to come together. As for the aircraft, the best I could do was to pick up a C-130. But it will be zero timed before the week is out. It's in Canada. When you're ready, just let me know. Do you have the crew lined out yet?"

"Not completely," Hendricks said. "But I don't think Robinson will have any problem picking up the flight crew. There are dozens of leftover bush pilots from the old Congo and Biafra days. Pay them well and they'll take anything anywhere."

For the next two hours, the conversation was about logistics and timing, trying to find ways to save a day or two and not jeopardize the operation. It didn't appear that there were any. The mission would have to progress at its own rate of development.

While they talked, Jameson packed Hendricks's bags, checked him out of his hotel and waited with the limo to take him to the airport. Next stop was Los Angeles and a visit with the hotshot director-producer.

They had a rough time frame: three weeks. During that time, there was much to do. In many ways, this was much more difficult to put together than their original raid. Before, they'd had the support of more than one government. Papers and arms as well as transport had been arranged so there would be no possibility of more than minor difficulties presenting themselves.

Not so this time. They had to do it all, and everything about the job was bogus. One slip and the entire house of cards would come falling in on them. If that happened, Duke and the others were truly lost.

It was near four in the afternoon when Hendricks left Collier for the ride back to Kennedy. The plane was an hour late getting off, because as usual things were stacked up in the traffic pattern. The best Hendricks could do—after making it clear to the stewardesses that he didn't want to watch the movie or eat—was catch up on some sleep. It was better than when he'd flown in. Jameson had booked his ticket and paid for it. He was going to the coast first class. He appreciated the extra room of the first class seats.

It was 0230 when he caught a cab from LAX. He had the driver take him to one of the motels off Century Boulevard that served the overnight airport trade, staying away from the more expensive hostelries. He needed his money for more important things than hotels. Even if Collier would pick up the check, it wasn't his way.

It was a sleep-drugged and weary voice that answered on the eleventh ring of the phone.

Hendricks said only, "I'm here. If you're not tied up, I'll meet you at noon at Frascatis on the strip."

Washington snapped to. Jones was left behind. "That'll work, Boss. Should I bring your old buddies over with me?"

"Yes, I'd like to see them again. Then it's twelve o'clock at Frascatis. You make the reservations."

"Right, Boss." The line went dead. Hendricks lay back in his bed and turned off the lights. For some reason, he felt better knowing that he'd fouled up Washington's sleep.

Hendricks arrived ten minutes early, mentioned the name of Mr. Jones of Redstar Productions to the maître d' and was shown immediately to a table for four.

He had just enough time for half a cup of coffee before Washington came in with Milton and Hooker.

They resisted the impulse to hug each other, though men embracing in public was not that unusual on the strip.

Hendricks asked them if they wanted to eat, then talk, or talk first.

The response was unanimous. He could see the curiosity and excitement in the way each controlled his reactions. Hooker developed a very slight tick on the right mandible where the muscles worked against each other. Milton was just tense, sitting too straight and bright-eyed. Washington was taking it the best, but then he'd been in from the beginning. Hendricks complimented him on how well he looked in lime-green linen and suggested they move into the bar. The restaurant was starting to fill, and it was too close to say much in there.

Washington shook off the maître d's inquiries about the service with "Everything's fine. It's just that I didn't know we'd be so pressed for time, and we need to talk in a bit more private surroundings."

Hendricks led the way to a table by the piano, which would not be used until the happy hour. The lounge was dark as always. He had picked this spot on Collier's recommendation, as it was a hangout for many of the movie types. Being there with Washington would not excite any curiosity; his status as a producer would give them cover.

"What's coming down for real, Boss?" asked Hooker. Milton nodded his head in agreement.

"Jones here filled us in some, but we still don't have it all. We're going to need it if we are going to be able to put this together."

Hendricks waited until each had drinks and the waitress had gone back to her station by the bar. "All right. This is it. We are going to do the biggest Trojan Horse yet. As of now we are looking at a time frame of about three weeks. Next week Washington— excuse me—Mr. Jones, I want you to have the public relations people from the studio contact the Bokalan Consulate and start the machinery going there. Put some heavy weight on them. You have to go to Bokala and interview Okediji yourself. You will do the recon. See everything, forget nothing. Remember you're going to make Okediji a star. An African Paul Newman. The Poitier of the bush.

"Once there, contact Kelo and try to put him in the pocket. Use whatever you think will work. We have the money if that's what he wants. We have talked about this before, and Kelo is playing some kind of game of his own. He doesn't give a shit about Okediji. That's all right. Maybe what we plan will work in with his thinking. I don't care what it is. Put him in our pocket somehow."

He turned his attention to Milton. "I want you to get ready to do some work. You will have to make our weapons look like those used in the studio, things that shoot blanks. But the adaptation has to be able to come off in seconds. In addition, I want you to make an adapter for blanks that will fit on AK, AKM and RPDs. Those are the standard light weapons used by Okediji's men. If this goes down right, there's a chance we can put most of his best men out of action before the first shot is fired."

Milton smiled happily. "I love it. Just point me to where I have to go, and I'll take care of them. How many weapons will I have to convert before we go operational?"

"About fifty. We'll have FALs, Uzis and a few MAGS, 7.62 NATO and 9mm."

"Piece of cake. I probably have enough adapters in stock now to handle that. All that will be required is a little tooling. Should I get the blank ammo, too? I know where to lay hands on it within the hour."

Hendricks took a sip of his drink, for the first time realizing what he had ordered. Scotch and soda with a twist. That was strange because he never drank it with a twist.

"Yes, anything that will save time. Also, you will

have to adapt a few grenades and some other hardware, just in case anyone looks at them too close. But I'll leave the complete list with Washington— damn it—I mean Jones, before I pull out."

One down. He turned to Hooker. "Now what about personnel? Any problem there?"

Hooker laughed cynically. "Are you kidding? There are more heroes in Hollywood than Fort Bragg or Camp Lejeune. I've gone through the old boy network here. All of them have some filmmaking experience. Gaffers, cameramen, a bunch of stunt men, all veterans, all bored with this plastic shit here. I've kept them apart. They don't know I'm recruiting for a job. But before the time comes, I'll interview each separately and replace any dropouts. These are good men.

"Either me or Milton have worked ops with each of them before. If they do drop out for any reason, they'll keep quiet. Especially when they hear there's a bonus for them if they do and some very angry friends who will come after them if they don't."

Hendrick's nodded, satisfied. "Good enough, George. You run that end. As for you Milt"—he turned his attention to the special effects man— "I'll want you in Guatemala within three days to start working on the weapons. I guess we can call them 'props,' can't we?"

He gave him Jameson's number, saying, "Arrange your flight through him. He'll contact me to let me know when you're coming in. Now listen up, everyone. We don't have any time to waste. Every day that we don't go, someone may die. Okediji is a crazy. He likes to cut and hurt people. He has already taken out some people you know and have worked with.

"Duke and Claude are both in prison in Bokala. If we don't do something fast, they will die there. You know Africa; they will not die quickly. So, let's get our shit together and keep things moving!"

FIFTEEN

Time. It was moving like old blood. Thick and sluggish. At least it seemed that way. Hendricks knew that was wrong. In real time they had moved mountains. Milton was ready to go. His passport was in order, though he didn't need one for Guatemala. Proof of citizenship was enough for a tourist card. When he left, Milton would go with him. Hendricks's biggest concern was whether or not Washington was going to be able to get into Bokala. Right now Washington was with Chalmers from the studio.

"Mr. Jones, I would like you to meet Jerome Forbes of the Forbes Agency. They handle our PR."

Washington shook hands with a man who had the look of someone who liked meat. Dead meat. Preferably old, dead meat. Washington thought that Forbes could probably make a very good living doing horror films. The eyes were cavernous and sick. The color of them was hard to distinguish. His clothes were West Coast pastel, which was totally out of place with the parchment-yellow skin that hung loosely on his bony frame.

After shaking hands, Washington wanted to either find a bathroom and wash his or go to the nearest sawmill and pick up several sharpened stakes.

Forbes's voice was surprisingly rich and forceful. His enunciation had a touch of the Brit to it: clipped, sure.

"Mr. Jones, Allison tells me you might have need of our services. All that I know at this time is that you are putting together a sizable package and have the full support of Mr. Collier, a man whom I greatly admire. Therefore I am, of course, at your service."

"I appreciate that, Mr. Forbes, and I do think we need someone with expertise in this matter. I need to go to the Republic of Bokala and to have a personal meeting with the president, Leopoldo Okediji."

Forbes didn't have the slightest idea where Bokala was or what kind of place this Okediji person was president of. He didn't care. In the past, he had dealt with heads of state from Europe and run election campaigns for governors, senators and two presidents. He didn't know who or what was occurring in Bokala, but he had people who would know very soon. From his Washington branch, he had the ability to access everything that was known about the consulate of Bokala and what their policies, if they had any, were at this time. He also knew how to arrange introductions with God if he happened to be in town.

"Very good, Mr. Jones. I'll get to work on it. It would make my job somewhat easier if I knew the purpose of the meeting. That is if it's not too confidential, of course. I think that Mr. Chalmers will assure you that I am the soul of discretion. In my work, one has to be."

Washington looked at Allison for confirmation, knowing full well that he would have to let the PR zombie in on the film idea.

Allison said as firmly as he could without being pushy, "Yes, of course. Jerome has handled many of our talents for us and has performed many useful functions for Mr. Collier. He and his office are registered lobbyists in the Capitol."

Allison Chalmers moved to his desk and removed a bound document of about forty pages.

"You requested this at our first meeting, and I am pleased to offer it to you at this time. If you decide it is the correct thing to do, then I would like Forbes to read it also. I think it will speak very clearly about what our intentions are concerning Bokala and President Okediji."

Washington knew that Allison was pushing him a bit, trying to assert his position in front of Forbes. Taking the document, he read the cover sheet with the grandiose title *Okediji, the Leopard of Bokala.*

It was the treatment.

Taking it to an overstuffed brown leather chair where he would have aid of a lamp to read by, Washington excused himself. "Yes, I see. Now, if you will grant me just a few minutes, I would like to go over this. However, Allison, I've every confidence, considering your history, that this will be exactly what we need."

He read rapidly, trying not to either laugh or gag at several points. It was what he needed. It made Okediji look as if he were the African version of Charlemagne: noble, self-sacrificing, a patriot of the highest order and morals. Okediji was going to love it. And if it worked right, it would kill him.

"Yes, yes. This is very good, Allison. I'm proud of you, and I know that Mr. Collier will be also. By the way, has Anthony come in yet?"

"Yes, he should have been here by now. I talked to him over the phone earlier, and he said that whatever you decided on this matter he would go along with. He has the greatest confidence in your judgment."

Washington nodded. "Very good, then I see no reason why Mr. Forbes should not read this. As you said, it will explain things quite well."

He handed the treatment over to Forbes, who removed a pair of bifocals, adjusted them on his thin nose and went through the treatment in less than three minutes.

Washington had no doubt the entire contents were fully and completely committed to memory. It was a known fact that vampires never forgot anything.

Removing his glasses and placing them back in a thin silver case, Forbes said, "I see. Yes. Well, the first thing to do is to observe protocol. I shall have my Washington office contact the consulate there. That is if they have one." He left that open as a question.

"They do," said Washington.

"All right. I should know something . . ." He checked his watch. ". . . within the hour, if you will permit me to use your phone to call my office, Allison."

"Yes, go right ahead. I know Mr. Jones feels this project requires speed. It is, as he said, a timely event and must be moved ahead as expeditiously as possible."

Washington agreed.

Forbes was on the phone when Anthony came in unannounced. He was, after all, the boss's son and could come and go where he pleased, when he pleased.

Allison came forward to greet him warmly. Washington admired that in a man. He certainly knew who to suck up to. Showed intelligence.

Anthony greeted Washington as an old friend, asking "How's it going?"

Washington pointed to Forbes on the phone. "We're making progress. He's checking the Bokalan consulate now. Says we have to go in that way."

"Then he's right," Anthony said. "Forbes is one of the best if not the best. If Forbes says this is the way to go, then he's right. Dad has the greatest confidence in his abilities. He's worked for my father for years."

Forbes set the phone down and turned back to the others, smiling as if a dinner plate full of fresh raw liver had just been delivered to him. Then he greeted Anthony.

"Anthony, good to see you again, my dear boy. And how is your father? As crude and shrewd as always, I presume?"

Forbes did truly admire Old Man Collier. Collier knew what he wanted and he got it.

"He's fine, Mr. Forbes, just fine, and I know that he will be pleased that you were able to come here today in person. We all know how busy you are."

"Nonsense, my boy. I always have time for old friends, which your father certainly is. I make it a point to personally supervise all of his transactions with my company."

Anthony knew that he did, too. "How are you doing on the Bokalan thing?"

Forbes inclined his head toward the phone. "I just

got off the line to my office in D.C. They should be right on it, I expect to hear something momentarily. In fact, I left them this number to call."

Forbes looked at Allison, knowing his answer before it was given, but then one must observe the niceties, otherwise all was chaos. "I do hope you don't mind, Allison."

"Not at all. Make yourself to home."

The conversation for the next half hour was bland. Everyone complimented everyone else on whatever it was they were doing. Chalmers had told his secretary to put through only calls for Forbes. When the call came, Forbes spoke on the line softly, intentionally keeping the others in suspense for about five minutes. Then he turned and set the phone back on its cradle.

"I am pleased to say that we have opened the door to the Bokalan Consulate. When our office explained what the purpose of your request was, the consul was, to use my man's words, falling over his ass to be helpful. He has just taken over the office there and doesn't know anything or anyone. His predecessor has disappeared.

"I have the feeling that this is the first piece of real business he has ever been involved with. Therefore, he says that if you will but give him a day's notice, he will set some time aside for you."

Washington looked at Anthony and winked. Then he said, "Very good. I am impressed and can see why Mr. Collier has such confidence in you. Now, as for time, day after tomorrow would work very nicely. Then, if there are no difficulties, I will fly immediately to Bokala for the interview. During that time, Allison, I would like to see the first draft of the shooting script put together, so that it will be ready when I return. You can do that, can't you?"

Allison looked at Anthony. With the boss's son present, he was not about to admit that anything was impossible.

"Of course. All I was waiting for was your approval of the treatment. I will have the writers get back on it immediately."

Anthony jumped in, adding his strength to the conversation.

"All right. I think things are moving along quite nicely. Mr. Forbes, if you will coordinate with Allison, he will provide your D.C. office with whatever documentation the Bokalans may need to make them confident that we are going to do a real class job on this project. Give them anything they need to reassure them. I will remain here to keep an eye on things while Jones goes to Bokala. If any questions concerning the project come in, please refer them to me before making a response of any kind."

Forbes observed the proceedings with amusement. He was very pleased with himself. He had anticipated what would be asked of him. That was one of the reasons for his long and continued success. He had already known about the script, this Mr. Jones and the plan to do the life story of Okediji. Nothing happened in this town that he did not find out about.

Of course, he had become more interested after Mr. Collier had called him personally and asked for him to assist his son in his new project. Once he knew there was a project, it did not require very much effort to find out what it was. Which reminded him he needed to see that Allison's secretary's son received his SAG card.

As for the Bokalan Consulate, he had put people on that nearly a week ago—contingency planning. If, as Allison's secretary had told him, they were going to go on location, they would need visas and that meant the consulate. It also meant that sooner or later he would be called in to handle the PR. Consulate, that was a joke. A cheap house shared by two other so-called consulates from the dark continent.

The new consul was like so many others from backwater nations. He didn't have any idea what he was supposed to be doing, which naturally made it easier for Forbes. His office, in anticipation of supplying some future services, had already arranged for the Bokalan consul—someone with the ridiculous name of Mahamet Nkuma—to be invited to the Washington Press Club for a dinner. The guest list included several foreign ministers as well as the American secretary of state.

No, indeed. He anticipated no problems on his end. He would deliver, but then he always did. That's why he got the big bucks. Plan ahead, don't look for things to happen, make things happen.

"Boss, things are starting to happen."

Anthony agreed with Washington, saying, "I feel better now that we have old Forbes on the team. He's a shrewd, calculating son of a bitch, but he gets things done. He always seems to be ready when you need him."

Washington shook his head affirmatively. "Yeah. I had the feeling that we weren't telling him anything he didn't already know. It was like he was ahead of us all the way."

Hendricks grunted. "Maybe he was. Anthony, do you think he's on to us?"

Young Collier shook his head. "No. But if he was, he'd keep quiet about it. His greatest love is money, and he has an annual retainer of over two hundred thousand from my father's main offices. He would slice his mother's throat open before he would give that up. I think he just got onto the film story idea, not the rest of it. But I'll check in with Dad. He'll make certain that Forbes doesn't get in the way."

Hendricks said flatly, "I hope so. We can't afford any leaks at this point or at any other."

Changing the subject, he told them, "I have talked with Robinson. He has most of the men lined up. The Dutchman gave him a little shit, but it's been squared away with a bonus. In addition, the Dutchman used to be active. He knows why we're going back in. He'll deliver the rest of the men on time. For me, it's back to Guate with Milton. He has a lot to do there, and I have to get Tono busy arranging the weapons drop on Grand Turk.

"Your next priorities are: For you Washington, get your ass over to Bokala as fast as possible and get back. Anthony, you keep the lid on things here. I have talked with Hooker and Milton; they know you're in. If they need anything, they are to come to you."

It seemed as if time was still dragging, but it was coming together. The weapons were secured. Transport was ready. The men were coming in, in less than three weeks if they were lucky. He only hoped that Duke and the others could hold out that long. If Washington could get to Okediji, he might be able get him to ease off of them.

SIXTEEN

Washington was grateful that the flight was over and even more so that he had been escorted through customs and immigration by two officers in full battle dress. They carried only side arms, but the presence of armed security was everywhere.

It had been a strange, heavy feeling that had rushed over him as he looked out the window of the F-27 and saw that the airfield was pretty much the same as when they had left it. The burned-out hulk of the C-130 had been bulldozed off to the side of the field. The Migs and other aircraft they'd taken out still sat where they had burned. Skeletal hulks, they now seemed to be the desiccated bones of prehistoric predatory birds, from a time long past and half-forgotten. The control tower was back in operation of sorts. The walls had not been patched on the tower or the terminal. The pockmarks from machine gun fire bore mute testimony to the fierceness of the battle fought here.

Inside, the fire damage to the terminal had been covered over roughly with several layers of a horrible off-green paint, but the scent of smoke still hung on, or was it his imagination?

The two officers, one of them wearing the pips of a major, had come to greet him. As he came out of the door of the Fokker, heat had washed over him. Instantly, sweat formed pockets under his armpits and beaded his forehead before running down into his eyes. Wiping his eyes clear with a blue silk handkerchief, he could see the distaste in the officers' eyes at his dress. Good! That was what he wanted. Let them think he was a fairy or soft. If they did that, they would not consider him a threat.

He was taken through immigration, where his passport was stamped quickly, giving him thirty days in the country. As this was being done, his two bags were taken directly from the plane by a soldier and left waiting for him at the customs table.

The major waved him through. He was the personal guest of President Leopoldo Okediji, and as such, there was no need for such trifles. As he was being taken through to the outside, several of the other passengers—Nigerians, Hindus, Moslems and a sprinkling of other types—gave him a dirty look.

Outside, the heat of the day hit him again. African heat. Memories of childhood. Red dust, wells that ran dry and the crying of dying animals and children. During the dry years, children had stood alongside the dirt road with tin pans to beg water from the occasional truck or car that passed through their village. Bad memory. He pushed it back down and away. He had to remember who he was: a film producer come to do an epic.

Outside the terminal, a five-year-old Mercedes was waiting for him. To the front and rear were ten-year-old Ford pickups filled with soldiers from the Palace Guard. They wore the splinter type Portuguese-pattern camouflage uniforms with the sleeves rolled up to their biceps. Each of them was armed with the People's Republic's version of the AKM, Kalashnikov assault rifle. Washington knew that they were usually of better quality than the original Russian-made guns.

The first pickup pulled out in front. Over the cab of the truck was a Leopard holding a shoulder-fired RPG-7 rocket-propelled grenade launcher pointing down the road. The troops in the back were sitting on makeshift wooden benches that faced out to the sides. Each man had his weapon at the ready and eyes on his side of the road. There was no grab-assing around. The truck in the rear was the same, with the exception that its lmg faced to the rear on a tripod.

The ride back into Bokala City was much different from the first time. Washington had a flashback when they went through the checkpoint where he had killed the sentries and Bone, a brother who had panicked.

It was curious how things looked different in the light. When they'd first come in, they'd had the night to cover them. A good part of the trip had been made with him and the other drivers wearing infra-red glasses, which changed lights and buildings into green, glowing phantoms.

He had to put his mind back on the job at hand. They pulled around the park to the front gate of the National Palace. In the harsh light of full day it looked tired, worn out. The former colonial glory was fast fading. It needed painting, and the grounds were going to seed and weed. Washington had not seen much traffic or even many people on the road coming in. Things were still severely disrupted.

They pulled into the circular driveway in front of

the palace. An armed guard opened the door for Washington. He had started to ask about his bags when the officer with the major's pips on the shoulders broke in.

"We will take your baggage to the hotel," he said. "The best suite has been reserved for you at the orders of the president."

He didn't sound much as if he enjoyed the chore, and Washington didn't really give a shit.

At the large double doors of the entrance, two more guards were wearing the same type of uniform as the other guards and carrying the ubiquitous AKMs. As Washington started up the steps, they snapped to attention, presenting arms. Behind them, carrying only side arms in canvas holsters, were two men in more or less a form of civilian dress, consisting of khaki shirts and pants, which were in need of repair and a good washing. These men asked to see Washington's passport. After one had carefully and laboriously entered Washington's name on a register, the other opened the door, turning him over to another military aide, who would escort him to the office of the president of Bokala, Leopoldo Okediji.

In the spacious former offices of Mehendi, the scars from the attack on the palace had mostly been patched or covered over, though Washington could see a line of recently painted-over pockmarks where machine gun fire had raked the room. Most of the National Palace was still closed off, unfit for use or show.

Washington relaxed as if he owned the place. His brilliant purple-and-gold Italian silk shirt, Bill Blass jeans and gold Rolex watch were in glorious contrast to the severe Portuguese pattern camouflage uniform of the man sitting across from him. Only four rows of ribbons and a scarlet sash, which ran from his right shoulder to his left hip, gave the uniform any color at all.

Okediji's face was drawn, tired. His mouth was set in a thin line, compressing his normally full, sensuous lips. His eyes had a touch of yellow in the whites, and he looked suspicious, if not vicious.

Their conversation had lasted over an hour, and Washington believed that Okediji was buying it. If he wasn't, then Washington knew he would never leave Bokala alive.

"Very good, Mr. President. I do believe we have covered most of the details. But I have just had what I think you will agree is a marvelous idea."

Okediji watched this Hollywood nigger with ill-concealed distaste.

"And what is that Mr. Jones?"

Leaning forward, Washington let cigarette ashes drop on the floor, marring the carpets from Bosra.

"It's a natural. As soon as we finish the filming of the battle scenes and tie up the loose ends, I think it would be a marvelous idea to tag the show with a parade of the actual prisoners. Now imagine this. The mercenaries will be paraded across an open field under the watchful eyes of your own palace guards. What do you call them? Your Leopards! Marvelous title. I love good titles, don't you?"

He leaned even closer, his voice dropping to a conspiratorial whisper. Okediji in spite of himself found he was leaning over across his desk to hear what was coming next.

"We will superimpose over all this, *your face* in

the African sky. Your eyes straight ahead, as if
looking into the future. You will be the spirit of the
times, the all seeing, the force behind the struggle of
Africa to free itself of the last vestiges of colonial
oppression and restore the pride of the African
peoples. You will be *Godlike*!"

Okediji found the image becoming. It wasn't too
far from the way he thought of himself. The things
he had achieved were almost supernatural. He had
thought at times that there were greater powers
guiding his hand. This butterfly in front of him, as
distasteful as he was physically, seemed to have an
insight that those around Okediji lacked. But perhaps that's why he was what they called an artist.

Yes, he could see it! A film like this would draw
the world's attention to him. It could open doors to
new areas of influence and power. He could become
the voice of Africa today.

Washington could see Okediji flush beneath his
dark skin and knew he'd sunk the hook. Ego had
destroyed better and worse men. Pursing his fingers
under his chin, he waited patiently till Okediji
cleared his throat and spoke.

"Yes, Mr. Jones. I think you have an excellent idea.
And this is the time to use all the modern communication facilities one can muster to achieve our
greater goal of a free Africa for Africans. I will issue
the necessary instructions and documents so that
you may proceed with your production. Is there
anything else that I can do for you at this time?"

"Why yes, Mr. President. I, as you know, live only
in a world of dreams and fantasy. I have never had
experiences such as you know."

Sighing deeply as if with a mixed feeling of envy

and regret, Washington continued, "But then we all have our talents and must live with what nature has given us."

Okediji waved his hand. He was beginning to get a bit irritated at the manner in which Jones kept stretching things out. "Yes, yes, of course, Mr. Jones. But what is it you wish for me to do at this time?"

Washington sucked at his upper lip, letting a breath of air out slowly, deliciously. "Why, Mr. President, I would simply die, I mean just roll over, if I could see the mercenaries you have captured. I have never seen a real one, you know. And it would help me in my casting to see what some of these people are really like."

Okediji shook his head back and forth. "I don't think so, Mr. Jones. Those men are under maximum security. No one sees them."

Washington leaned back as an expression of extreme disappointment came across his face. "That is regrettable, Mr. President, because I certainly feel that it is necessary for me to see and even talk to one or two of them. If this production of your story is to come alive for the world to see, I must be allowed a little freedom to do those things I think are vital to the production, even though you may not agree with them.

"Remember, you are the man, but I am the artist who will paint the picture of the man. And I am the one who is putting millions of dollars at risk to bring you and your story to the world."

Okediji was not so much worried simply that Jones would see or talk to the prisoners. It was their physical condition that worried him.

"Very well, Mr. Jones. I will submit to the artist.

However"—he checked his desk calendar—"today is Thursday. You will not be able to see them until Saturday. At which time I will instruct Commander Muslama at the prison to give you whatever assistance you need." This would give Okediji a few days to get the prisoners cleaned up and looking better cared for.

Washington rose to his feet. "Why, that is absolutely perfect, Mr. President. I will need a bit of time to prepare my thoughts and notes. One thing more, I will need a personal liaison with your office. A person with sufficient intelligence and authority to see that we do not have problems with parking tickets and such when we are on the move. You understand, of course."

Okediji didn't want to tell him that in Bokala they did not give out parking tickets because there weren't any printed.

"Yes, yes, most certainly, a liaison officer, by all means, Mr. Jones. I have just the man for you. Intelligent, well educated. I think he will be a great value to you. I will have him come to your hotel. Would seven this evening be suitable?"

Washington flipped a quick look at his Rolex. "Yes, that would be perfect. I will wait for him in the lounge. Do you think he will be able to recognize me? Or should I wear a flower in my lapel or something?"

Okediji turned his back, letting loose of a deep sigh, "No, Mr. Jones, I do not think he will have any trouble spotting you. Now, if you will excuse me, I do have a country to run."

Washington swished himself out of the office and onto the street, where the president's limo was waiting to take him back to his hotel. It was a fight all the way back. It was not until he was in his hotel, in the bathroom, with the water running, that he was finally able to let loose the laughter that had been building inside of him all afternoon.

The rest of the afternoon, Washington relaxed in his room. It was too hot to think about eating. The best he could do was lie on the bed in his underwear and watch the overhead fan rotate feebly in a futile effort to move the air around the room.

At six he took a lukewarm shower—not by choice; lukewarm was all they had. It came from a tank on the roof heated by the sun, but it at least rinsed off the sweat. Outside he could hear activity picking up on the streets as the sun set—street vendors and food stalls on the sidewalks.

It was still too early for the street whores to be out. But they would appear in the next couple of hours. Everyone was trying to sell something, anything, in order to eat. The price for the girls ranged from fifty cents American for a quickie to ten U.S. dollars for a night with the best. A sign of the times, but even at the bargain prices there would be few takers. The rate of exchange for Bokalan francs was sixteen thousand to one at the bank and twenty percent more on the street.

It took Washington nearly the rest of the hour to dress. Rodeo Drive would have been proud of him. Yellow silk shirt, white Egyptian cotton trousers and deck shoes. These were set off with enough gold chains and bracelets to make a New York pimp cry with envy.

This was the apparition that Okediji's liaison

officer saw when the door to Washington's room opened.

Kelo's expression began to crack first around the edges, then the corners of his mouth, and finally his entire face broke out in a grin, which showed a full, strong set of white teeth.

Washington grabbed Kelo's hand and pulled him inside. He wanted to say something but thought it best to play the role a bit longer. There was always a chance that the room was bugged. If he'd been Okediji, it would have been.

"Oh yes, Major Kelo, I believe. We were to meet in the lounge, but this will work very nicely, I think. No, in fact, let's go and get something cool to drink. Then we can discuss business."

Kelo covered his mouth with his hand for a moment, wiping away the smile and the beginning of a laugh.

"Certainly, Mr. Jones. His excellency has instructed me to give whatever assistance you may require."

Standing aside, Kelo let Washington pass him and closed the door behind him. They walked down the two flights of stairs to the main floor rather than take a chance on whether or not the elevator would work. Neither man talked until they had found their way to a postage stamp–sized table in the corner of the lounge.

The hotel had at one time been a Holiday Inn lookalike, but time and lack of maintenance and customers had given it an abandoned feeling. There were only two other customers, an East German sitting with a hack from some ministry or other.

Their heads were close together as if the two were cutting some kind of deal.

The bartender was bored and didn't care if he served drinks or not. Kelo snapped his fingers for the bartender's attention, and with great reluctance he ambled slowly over to the table.

When he saw the gold hanging from Washington's neck and wrists, his eyes opened slightly, revealing red rims where the whites should have been. His mind went immediately to some people he knew who would love the chance to liberate the gold from this American slave nigger.

Kelo saw the interest in the bartender's eyes, the first sign of life he'd shown since they'd come in. Crooking his finger, Kelo signaled for him to come closer. Half leaning over, Kelo said softly, "Don't even think about it."

The bartender started to straighten back up, protesting. "Think about what, sir?"

Kelo's left hand reached out around the back of the man's neck, pulling his face nearly to the level of the table. A 9mm Browning appeared in Kelo's right hand, the barrel resting directly under the bartender's nose. The sound of the hammer being cocked brought the German's and the black's heads around. Seeing the events at Washington's table, they hastily made an exit without paying their bill.

Kelo pressed the pistol deeper into the sensitive flesh of the man's upper lip.

"I said don't even think about it. If anything happens to this gentleman, then you are going to die. He is under the personal protection of the president, and I am the president's representative. Now, bring us two beers, cold ones, and clear your mind, or I

will do it for you, and we will serve ourselves while
the management looks for a new bartender."

The bartender's attitude changed at once. He was
all attention and sincerity. He began to make ex-
cuses and denials, all the time bobbing his head up
and down faster and faster. Kelo stopped him with a
curt bark.

"Stop that, you fool, or I will kill you just to
remove the stupid expression from your face. Now
go!"

Backing away, still bowing and apologizing for any
unintentional misunderstanding, the bartender retreated to the bar, dreading the fact that he would
have to go back to the table with the beers.

Washington and Kelo would wait and talk after
they had been served. They ignored the bartender as
he placed the beers on the table. Once he had
retreated out of earshot, all the while avoiding their
eyes, Washington began.

"Kelo, it's good to see you again. But you certainly
are not making any friends for the government."

Kelo laughed softly. "I do not wish to make friends
for Okediji. But, to more important matters—once I
saw you in the hallway of the palace, I knew that
Hendricks was coming back. But why this act? What
are you planning?"

Washington took a pull of the beer, made a face at
the taste and pushed the glass away. It tasted soapy.

"Right. Hendricks is coming back. I was going to
contact you as soon as I could anyway. But this is
much better, since Okediji's assigning you to me will
make it much easier for us to meet. In fact, we
will probably spend a great deal of time together. But
I have to ask you to explain some things before I can

tell you any more. First, we don't know why you helped us escape or why you feel you owe Hendricks something, but will you help us again? It might get bloody. In fact, I guarantee it will. Second, we want to know why you would help us again after helping to overthrow Mehendi in the first place. Isn't this what you wanted?"

Kelo smiled easily; his eyes moved around the interior of the room. The bartender's gaze touched his for a second, and the other man fled into the kitchen. Washington and Kelo were alone.

"I know, Washington, that it must seem strange to you that I would help you when I went to so much effort to have the forces of Okediji take power. Let us just say that I have some long-range plans and this was just the first move. I will do what I can to bring Okediji down, as I did Mehendi."

Kelo pushed his own beer away untasted.

"All I can tell you is I have my own reasons," he said. "It is true that I feel nothing personally for the men in the prison, but that is not my concern. It is the concern of you and Hendricks, but not me. I do not personally care if they live or die. They mean nothing to me except if they can help me achieve my own ends. They are, after all, nothing more than hired killers."

Washington began to get a clue as to Kelo's thinking.

SEVENTEEN

Hendricks and Milton came into Guatemala on TACA Airlines, leaving L.A. at 2300 and arriving in Guatemala at 0630. They would spend only one day and night in the city, where Hendricks would meet once more with Tono and Ponce.

Magic Milton was ready and eager to get to work. He had brought with him everything they needed and more. They'd cleared immigration and their luggage had come on the line. Hendricks knew that it would be a problem if the customs people got too curious about some of the strange-looking things that they were bringing into the country.

Often, customs people in the tropics became paranoid, but Hendricks knew how to deal with that. Instead of waiting for them to inspect his luggage and the three trunks that belonged to Milton, he asked one of the airport *Guardia de la Hacienda* security people, who were standing around the terminal wearing side arms, to call the military representative. In the airport, this was always an officer of the air force, and Hendricks knew many of them, including Waller, their Commanding General.

As he and Milton waited for the military representative, crowds of homecoming Chapinas pushed past them carrying suitcases large enough for families of refugee Cubans to live in. These were stuffed with hard-to-get items: hair dryers, toasters and VCRs. If that had been all he was trying to get by customs, Hendricks wouldn't have worried about it. But the customs people didn't turn a tolerant eye on anything with a military or weaponish look to it. That was given over to the military immediately.

It took a few minutes before the *Guardia de la Hacienda* type in his gardener-green uniform and peaked cap came back, guiding a *Fuerza de Aereo* officer in civilian dress. Captain Garcia's eyes lit up when he saw Hendricks.

"*Ola, amigo.* What are you smuggling in this time? More sniper rifles?"

He had been on duty last year when Hendricks had brought in half a dozen rifles for his sniper training program in Quiché. He had turned the weapons over to Garcia, then left and came back the next day with a note from the Ministry of Defense authorizing Garcia to turn the weapons over to him.

Since then, there had been several other times when he had brought in items of a military nature. While Garcia had not been on duty for every such occasion, he knew when they happened. For each time thereafter, Hendricks nearly always made it a point to bring a couple of boxes of 9mm with hot loads for Garcia. He was on the Guatemalan shooting team and was always short of ammo.

Garcia pointed at the trunks. "Are these yours?"

Hendricks affirmed that they were and that he'd like for them to be put back in the air force's office until he returned with the release for them the next day.

Garcia gave an order, and three porters hustled

over to haul the trunks back to his office, which was just the other side of immigration.

Once they had been put inside, Garcia tapped one of them with his foot. "Anything interesting in there?"

Hendricks laughed pleasantly. "Not for you. You won't believe it, but the things in there are designed to make guns shoot blanks."

Garcia shook his head. Hendricks was right; he didn't believe it. But then no one in Guatemala, where there had been a guerrilla war going on for twenty years, could possibly see any reason to bring into the county something that did not shoot real bullets.

"Okay, Señor Hendricks. Whatever you say. I will be on duty tomorrow until three in the afternoon. If you can come for your things that do not shoot before then, I will release them to you. Providing, of course, you can get permission to bring them in. I don't think the general will be happy with them, though. Are you certain you do not have at least one flame thrower in there? It would make him easier to deal with."

He, Hendricks and Milton all laughed at the joke.

Garcia escorted them back to the customs line and signaled the agent with his finger. They shook hands all around, then Hendricks and Milton stepped into line. When their turn came, the agent looked at them curiously and stamped their bags without inspecting them.

Tino was waiting for them with the Samurai. As it was still too early for anyone to be doing any business, they drove straight on to the house, where

Alejandra fixed breakfast, then took naps for two hours and headed back to town by 1100.

Hendricks was able to meet with Ponce after lunch and obtain the permit to take Milton's trunks out with no problem. General Ponce had also anticipated one of his requirements and had already waiting for him a document that would let him into the military warehouse at Puerto Barrios, where the weapons were now in storage. Everything else was in order. Hendricks gave Ponce Collier's number in New York so he could confirm the purchase and subsequent shipment of the medical package. Ponce denied his need for such reassurance, but Hendricks knew it would make him more at ease. Ponce knew who Collier was. Collier had business enterprises covering the globe, and some of them were involved with the purchase of sugar and coffee, both of which were large export items for Guatemala.

After that he met with Tono to get him lined up on the Grand Turk situation. Tono was eager to go to work on the setup. He had not been there for some years, and the chance of a free vacation on a tropical island appealed to him. Especially because he could take with him one of his legion of girl friends to keep him company, far from the jealous eyes of his wife. That and ten thousand dollars were sufficient to insure that he would do his very best to arrange things to Hendricks's satisfaction.

Though, to be truthful, Tono saw no problem. He had been assured that there would be available a liberal amount of what the Chinese call the "fragrant grease" to smooth the way with any reluctant officials.

When Hendricks had finished with Tono, it was

back to the house to sleep through till the next
morning.

They left at dawn. It was a long drive to Puerto
Barrios, not in time so much as in horror. The
hundred miles of road were not the best, and the
traffic would have given a Samurai bent on *seppuku*
bad dreams. As soon as they dropped off the plateau,
they came into El Rancho at the entrance to Gaute-
mala's only desert. Not much of a desert by American or African standards, but it reminded one of the
Mojave. It was only about twenty miles wide and
about thirty miles long. To the south was Honduras;
to the north was the Alta Vera Paz, where much of
the best coffee was grown in the cool highlands.

It took five hours for them to reach Puerto Barrios.
There, Hendricks checked into the Puerto Libre
motel, owned by Rudy Bodner, a German friend of
his. As far as Hendricks knew, this was the only
motel in the area with air conditioning. That was
helpful if you were not acclimated.

Once past El Rancho, the climate became increas-
ingly subtropical, and Puerto Barrios was the perfect
image of a banana republic port: wood frame buildings, nearly all of them faded to where the bare wood
was showing through, gray and unhealthy looking.
The flaking paint that still clung stubbornly in
sun-bleached patches was in the usual panorama of
colors favored by Latinos: a green *mercado* selling
hardware next to an orange cantina. The many
unpaved streets turned into slick quagmires during
the rainy season.

They spent the night at the Puerto Libre, taking
advantage of the pool and the food. Rudy had once

been a restaurant caterer in the States and had passed on his culinary skills to his kitchen staff. The food was always good, and the dining area, as well as the rooms, was clean and free of excessive animal life.

At eight the next morning, they drove into town, past the painted statue of a dockhand with a stem of bananas on his shoulders. Coming into the center of town, right off the main market they saw the bars and whorehouses, which catered to sailors on the cargo ships and coastal traders that put in to load sugar, coffee and bananas.

The army had a base there, as well as the navy. It was to the army base Hendricks went, to present Milton and his credentials to Colonel Lima, who reminded Hendricks of Ponce, except that he didn't have a mustache. Hendricks was glad to see him because Lima had been the commandant at the base at Santa Cruz del Quiché when he, Duke and Becaude had run their sniper program. It was always easier dealing with someone you knew and respected.

Hendricks didn't know what was in Ponce's letter to Colonel Lima, but it must have been strong. After reading it, Lima said, "*Esta bien*, Martin. When you are ready, I will show you to the warehouse where your boxes are waiting." His grayish eyes sparkled with curiosity. He would have given much to know what was coming down, but he was too polite to ask.

As he folded the letter up, putting it in his pocket instead of on his desk to be filed, he picked up the phone and spoke rapidly in Spanish. Milton heard the name Gramaho twice, but that was all he caught.

Lima hung up, and looking back to Hendricks and Milton, he said, "Martin, you know, of course, that officially those boxes and what is in them do not exist. This, as far I am concerned, is purely a social visit. You wanted to come down and have a drink with me and see about us going fishing out on the Cayos de Belice."

Getting up from his desk, he opened the center drawer and took out a ring of keys, then put on his American-style field cap and took Hendricks and Milton to the door of his office.

"I will personally take you and your friend over to the warehouse," he told them. "Your crates are the only items in storage there. You, Señor Milton, will be completely alone. I will put you in, and you will stay there until five o'clock. Today, I will have food sent over from our mess, but personally, I do not recommend it for a steady diet. Therefore I suggest you bring a lunch with you beginning tomorrow.

"If for any reason I am called on to a commission, or I am late or do not return, my aide, Captain Gramaho, will have orders to release you. Excuse me if that sounds as if you are under arrest. No, Captain Gramaho has orders to let you out. I do not plan on being detained, but one never knows for certain what is going to happen. So if you, Hendricks, come back for him at five, one way or the other he will be waiting for you."

Captain Gramaho was waiting for them as they stepped out into the heavy heat. The air had the smell of rain to it.

Gramaho clicked his heels to attention as Colonel Lima made the introductions and gave him his orders. He walked with them a short distance to where three rough buildings in need of primary maintenance stood desolate and alone.

Not completely, though, Hendricks saw two sentries move out of the shadows to snap to attention and salute as their commandant approached them. Lima returned the salute and handed Gramaho a ring of keys.

"Captain, I shall turn matters over to you."

Turning to Hendricks and Robinson, he said, "Enjoy yourselves, gentlemen. I hope to see you when I return—perhaps a bit of dinner this evening?"

Hendricks shook his head. "Sorry, Colonel. But I will have to get back to Guate as soon as possible. But,"—and he said this in Spanish—"I will leave Mr. Milton here until his work is complete. After that, I would be very grateful if you could arrange transport for him back to the capital."

"*Por su puesto*, of course, Martin. As you say, no problem."

Lima left Milton to his own devices under the care of Captain Gramaho, who opened the door to warehouse number three, then stood aside. He would not go inside unless invited, which he was not. He took no offense. This was a security matter, and he had no need to know.

Hendricks told Milton, "You go ahead and get a look. I'll bring the Jeep over with your gear."

Captain Gramaho was a darkly handsome man of mixed Indian and Spanish blood with the look of one who had seen more than his share of the jungles and mountains of Central America. He excused himself by pointing to the side of the warehouse, where one of the sentries was on duty.

"I will wait over there until Hendricks returns.

After he leaves, I am ordered to lock you in. I will return only to bring your lunch and release you at exactly five this evening."

The heat inside the warehouse was oppressive. The first thing Milton did was go around and open up some of the shuttered windows to let some air inside. Then he turned to the crates and began to hum to himself. By the time Hendricks came back and they'd pulled Milton's trunks inside, Milton had already gone over in his mind what had to be done.

"Piece of cake. On the FALs, all I have to do is replace the flash hider with this." He showed Hendricks a tube device with a matchstick-sized bore.

"This will trap enough gases to work the action and doesn't look too different from the real thing." He laughed. "Of course I guess it really doesn't matter if they look a bit different. I was just thinking movies again."

Hendricks looked around at the goods that were there. Assault rifles, Uzis, magazines and machine guns, everything he had ordered was lying there waiting for Magic Milton's touch.

"What about the Uzis?" asked Hendricks.

"Little tougher, but not much. I'll have to rework a few of them. Take off the barrels and put on new ones with an integral gas device. Those will be the ones we show off. The others will look the same, except the plug will come out in two seconds when you want to restore the weapons to operation. But they will look just like the dummys."

"Good enough. I'll leave it to you then and get on back to the capital. I have some calls to make. How long do you think you'll need here?"

Milton screwed his face up as he thought. "Well,

to change over fifty plus weapons, I would guess today and tomorrow."

"Very good, old boy, I will leave you to your own 'devices' till then."

Milton smiled at the bad joke.

"Okay, you go on, and when I'm done, I'm to let the colonel—What was his name, Lima?—know, and he'll arrange transport for me back to the city. Is that right?"

"Yes. But if you need to spend another day here, go ahead. Enjoy the pool at Bodner's. And if you like, they have a fairly good selection of girls here, and gringos are popular."

Hendricks left Milton and climbed back into the Samurai for the long ride back to the city. He wanted to get away as early as possible. He hated the long climb up from El Rancho, especially at night when you would come around a hairpin curve and be on the ass of a semi without taillights.

Between El Rancho and Guate, he had once counted over a hundred crosses on the sides of the road, each meaning that at this place at least one person had been killed. It averaged out to a cross for every kilometer.

EIGHTEEN

One more link in the chain was being put together. Now for Tono and the transport arrangements. If that went well, they would be ready to start moving. Right now Hendricks was tired. Deep, bone-weary tired. For the last month, it seemed as if he had not had one full night's sleep, what with travel and the multiple changes of time zones, the worry and doubts.

It all drained him. He needed to rest, and he knew it. Exhaustion clouded the mind and made it difficult to make decisions correctly. He could afford no mistake because his mind was drugged from lack of rest. He would close his eyes and rest for one night. Sleep deep and well. Then he would be able to push again.

Tino had just started the fire going when Hendricks nodded at him and smiled wearily. "*Ya me voy a cama*, Tino. *Pase un buen noche*," he said.

Tino wished the *jefe* a good evening, too, and a deep rest. He was worried by the deepening lines in the *jefe*'s already thin face. The gray eyes seemed to be washing out even more. The *jefe* needed to sleep. Tino wished he would take a woman. That would ease much of his strain.

Hendricks lay down between clean, crisp sheets,

freshly ironed by Alejandra, an incredible luxury.
Even as his eyes closed, he felt a rush of guilt,
wondering how his men in the dungeons of Bokala
were sleeping. The thought faded as nothingness
took him down.

As he slept, others were at work in Belgium and
Africa, in Los Angeles and New York. The process
had begun and could for a time move on under its
own volition.

Tono was at dinner with the minister of transport
and aviation for the island of Grand Turk. By the
time after-dinner drinks were served, an agreement
had been made and ten thousand dollars exchanged.
The minister had agreed because of the good relations he had always had with the Republic of Guatemala and because of his great sympathy for their
struggle against the communist terrorists.

He would not be concerned if a cargo was brought
into the duty-free area of his country to remain for
some days, possibly a week or two, then be taken
out. He would also not be upset if there were no
records kept of the transfer taking place. He would
use a trustworthy man from his office to insure that
there would be no difficulties, and the cargo would
be stored in one of his own warehouses. That would
cost only another five thousand dollars, to be paid
when the boxes were taken off his island. To what
destination, he didn't ask and didn't care.

He and Tono had done business in the past and
understood each other quite well. Sarda was into
something, obviously some form of contraband. But
that was not the minister's concern. Contraband
was a way of life in the Caribbean. It put food on

many plates and cars in many garages, including his.

Without the contraband trade, the minister believed, many of his people would have starved in abject poverty. Therefore, keeping their interests in his heart, he would permit this small transaction to take place and share his good fortune with his people by buying a new swimming pool for his beach house. His wife had been nagging him for one for the last three years.

Tono assured the minister that he and no one else would handle the situation, and he would come back two or three days before the shipment was due in and bring the cash with him. This would also enable him to have another few days of holiday at Hendricks's expense.

The minister excused himself and left Tono and his girl friend, Dolores Valdez, to enjoy the marimba band and tropical night.

In Brussels, Robinson did not have time to enjoy the quaint beauty of the city with its Flemish buildings and monuments. He was locked up with the Dutchman. As Tono dined with his lady, Robinson was having bad coffee and croissants with the Dutchman in his office.

The next candidate was due in five minutes.

The Dutchman had gone to fat over the years. The trim, blond-haired, blue-eyed boy who had served with the Walloon regiment of the Freiwilligen SS and after that with half a dozen mercenary armies around the world, had turned into a bulging, balding trader in human lives.

Power was still obvious, and Robinson saw, under the layers of fat, more brute physical strength than he would ever possess, if he worked out every day of his life. There was raw force in the Dutchman's heavy, sloping shoulders and thick neck.

Robinson wondered what his real name was or if he even had one. He had never heard him referred to as anything but the Dutchman. He was an old-line mercenary, and there was cruelty in his thick-lidded, pale eyes. Hendricks had said that he was also in his way loyal—but only to fighting men.

To many of those he contracted out, he was almost a father. He always referred to them as his boys. He could be trusted to pay out death benefits when one of his contracts fell. He never stole, and he never forgave or forgot anyone who did. Those few who had stolen from him in the past always paid their debt in one manner or another.

Hendricks, he liked. He had filled several orders for him over the years. Sometimes the jobs had been very risky, such as the Bokala raid. But Hendricks always made it clear up front what the odds were. He pulled no punches. Then if one of the Dutchman's boys wanted to sign on, it was on his head and luck.

Nothing had changed. He would get the men Robinson needed, and he wanted it to work. He had been a prisoner in Russia for eight years. He knew what it was like. If there was any way to get his boys out, he would go for it. Even if—and he hated think of it—it cost him his normal commission. Fortunately, that would not be the case with Hendricks. Somewhere he had found another backer, and the money was there.

The Dutchman liked Robinson, too. He was not a type one often found in this line of work. He was a bit too gentle, too—what was the word?—ahh yes, regular. Hendricks had told the Dutchman that Robinson had been in Bokala with him and had done well. It was enough.

Men came to this soldier's world for many reasons, and most died if not in combat then in their souls. For it was a drug that could not be cleansed out. It would, in time, consume you, burn you up. And the day would come when there was no longer any place for you. You were too old, too crippled or too drunk to be of value anymore.

The Dutchman had escaped that fate by making himself a broker. He did not go operational anymore, but he was still around the business and knew everything that was happening or going to happen.

There was a knock on the door. The Dutchman said, "*Kommen sie,*" and it opened to admit a man in his mid-thirties. As with most of the candidates, it would have been hard to mistake him for anything but a soldier. He had the look. The way he moved and stood—shoulders squared; hair dark brown, cut short and Prussian; eyes steady; looking ahead—he was almost at attention without being called to it.

"Good to see you, Stefan. Do you want to go to work?" asked the Dutchman.

Stefan answered sharply, "*Zum befehl.*"

"Please, sit down. You should meet this gentleman here. He has a proposition to put to you."

Stefan Marcyzk bowed his head slightly in Robinson's direction as the Dutchman introduced them.

"First, Stefan, I should tell you that the job will be with Martin Hendricks. This man is his representative."

The Dutchman turned the interview over to Robinson, saying, "As with the others, he knows the terms and conditions of the contract. However, I know this man much better than most of the others. He is good and steady. His history is excellent. If you accept him, he should be at least one of your squad leaders."

"Thanks, Dutchman. I will keep that in mind," Robinson replied.

"Now, Mr. Marcyzk, I accept the Dutchman's analysis of your worth. He has, I know, much more experience in that area than I do. Therefore, I will cut through to the proposal."

Stefan's eyes lit up. There was a deep spark in them. Robinson wasn't sure if they were brown or hazel. They seemed to change with his mood.

"Mr. Marcyzk, the job is a rescue. We are going into a Central African country to—" He never got to finish the sentence.

"You are going after the prisoners in Bokala. I am with you if you want me," Stefan interrupted.

"That's right. Bokala. I can't give you the details now. That will have to wait until we are operational, too late for anyone to back out or get sick. There can be no leaks on this, or everything will go down bad. But how did you know it would be Bokala?"

Stefan smiled, a thin-lipped smile. "The Dutchman said it was Hendricks's job. This is a small business. We know who the players are and where they play. As for my rapid response, suffice it to say that I have some friends in that prison and would like to get them out. Therefore, I am in."

"Mr. Marcyzk, I am somewhat new at this line of work. Tell me a bit about yourself."

Stefan looked at the Dutchman, who shrugged his

shoulders as if to say, "Tell him what you wish, that is your business."

Stefan looked steadily at Robinson. "All I can tell you is that I was born in Yugoslavia. I was in the army there. I left Yugoslavia and have traveled much. I speak German, French and English fluently. I am an expert with light weapons, both Western and Soviet Bloc.

"I have served on seven other missions, of different natures, some of them in Africa. As to who were my employers, I reserve the right to keep that information confidential. However, when next you speak to Hendricks, he will know who I am and my history. I was on two of those operations under his command."

Robinson nodded his head, satisfied. The man wasn't going to give anything away, and if the Dutchman vouched for him and he wasn't afraid to have Hendricks know his name, then he was all right.

"Very good, Mr. Marcyzk. As far as I am concerned, you are in. From this moment on, you are in isolation. I do not think it will be more than two weeks before we go into operational profile. However, as of now, you are mine. I presume you have followed the Dutchman's instructions and are ready to travel?"

Stefan stood up, going to full attention for the first time. "Yes, sir. I have my bags outside and have made the necessary arrangements so that I could leave for an indefinite period without any questions being asked. My passport is in order, and I am yours."

"Good. In that case, I shall take the Dutchman's

suggestion. As of this time and until you hear different, you will be in charge of the men waiting outside in the green Citroen vans. You are the last. Go and make yourself known to the others. I shall be with you in a few minutes."

Stefan answered crisply, "Yes, sir." He rose, made a short half bow to the Dutchman and to Robinson and then quick-marched back out.

After the door had closed behind him, the Dutchman turned to Robinson. "You made a good choice," he said. "When he was in the Yugoslav army, he was a major. He also knows and likes Hendricks very much. Hendricks will be pleased that you were able to get him."

Robinson said, "I hope so, but I'm glad that this is over. Now to settle your account, one thousand dollars a man. That's twenty thousand, including the Canadian flight crew. How do you want it handled?"

From his desk drawer the Dutchman took out a card with a series of numbers on it. "Have the funds transferred to this account here in Brussels."

Robinson put the card in his wallet and rose from his chair. It had been a long two days. They had gone through eighteen men before Stefan made his appearance. Of those, twelve had been accepted and, with Stefan, were waiting for him in the vans. For the next two weeks, or until Hendricks gave the word to rendezvous, they would all be in isolation doing PT, Robinson included, with the exception that he would be able to make periodic calls to Hendricks for progress reports. Other than that, he was going to be very bored and frustrated, especially when the memory of his travel agent in Guatemala came to mind, which only occurred about every five minutes. But then, as they say, war is hell.

Washington was in the jeep heading out to the airfield with Kelo. Once Okediji had given the order to cooperate with Mr. Jones, everything became incredibly easy. Especially when Kelo was with him. Washington was permitted to go anywhere he wished and to photograph anyone and anything. It was easy enough to explain his reasons for wanting to take pictures. They would be needed for his people in Hollywood. There would be some sets to build, and it would help with the script if the writers could see the actual layout of the airfield and other possible shooting locations.

And take pictures he did. With the automatic loader on his Nikon, he shot five rolls of film at the airfield alone. With Kelo driving him around, it took only a few minutes for the guards at the airfield to learn they were not to interfere with him in any way.

As they had driven up to the terminal, Washington had started taking some shots when the camera was jerked out his hand by an overeager Leopard captain.

The man found himself staring down the barrel of Kelo's Browning Hi-Power, the hammer cocked. "You stupid fool. Do you now who I am?" Kelo shouted.

The Leopard captain stupidly bobbed his head up and down, his eyes never leaving the bore of the pistol.

Kelo continued, his words dripping venom. "Then, you should know that anyone who is with me has approval. And do you know who gave approval for this man to take photographs of anything he wishes to. Do you? You stupid dog!"

The Leopard captain shook his head in the negative. He just couldn't find the strength to respond verbally as the bore followed his every movement.

"I know you don't, you fool. It is by the order of His Excellency Leopoldo Okediji, that is who, and you know that I am the president's aide, do you not?"

Again the stupidly bobbing head. The Leopard was ready to agree to anything if only Kelo would move the pistol away from where it intersected with the space between his eyes.

Kelo let the hammer of the Browning back down slowly. A sigh of relief escaped through the full lips of the captain as Kelo did so.

"Then, Captain, I suggest that you also inform everyone around here, and anywhere else you can think of, that this man is not to be offended or interfered with even if I am not with him. He has important work to do, and what that work is is none of your business. Obey orders and stay alive. For if this happens again, I will make you personally responsible, and you know what that means, don't you?"

The captain snapped to attention, saluting. "Yes, sir, I understand. Quite clear, sir. It was just a mistake. I was only trying to do my duty."

Kelo smiled at him evilly as if he were already seeing a dead man.

Very softy he said, "Good, good. You just keep on doing your duty. Now get out of the way. I have no more time for fools. We have much to do."

The Leopard still stood at attention, saluting with one hand while the other waved for the gate to the runway area to be lifted.

As Kelo and his passenger drove through, the Leopard felt as if he had been granted a reprieve. He cursed himself for being so stupid. But when Kelo had driven up, all he had seen was the strange man in the stranger clothes taking pictures, and he had strict orders concerning photographs of the airfield. He should have looked closer and seen who the driver was. He felt fortunate that Kelo had not killed him where he stood. He had the power to do that. He was the Barber's new "razor."

As they drove onto the tarmac, Washington cheerfully took pictures of everything. As he paused to reload the Nikon, he said, "As I told you before, you certainly have a way of making friends around here."

Kelo laughed and turned to take Washington to where the last stand of the mercenaries had been made in the ruins of the machine shop.

"Whatever," Kelo said. "But the word will go out faster than a jungle drumbeat. Within hours, every officer and most of the regular soldiers will know they are not to interfere with the 'Hollywood Nigger.' That's what Okediji called you." Looking at Washington in his rose-colored pima cotton safari suit, Kelo shook his head.

"I don't usually agree with Okediji about anything," he said, "but in this case, I think he came up with an incredibly accurate description of you. Do you dress this way in America?"

To tell the truth, Washington was a bit wounded.

He did like the clothes he'd bought. He thought the colors suited him, but he couldn't admit that to Kelo.

"No way, José. This is just part of my cover."

In New York, Jameson, following Collier's instructions, was shuffling money around to the proper accounts. It was no problem. The company, through its foreign office, had assets to draw from that could never be traced. It was all a matter of numbers. He flew to Switzerland himself, and at the branch office of their bank in the airport, he made the necessary transactions and transfers.

He didn't even have to clear customs, as the Swiss, in their thoughtfulness, had put their branch banks in the international section of the airport. While waiting for your next flight, you could take advantage of their services and never have a Swiss entry stamp in your passport. Very convenient.

It was through these transactions that the medical supplies for General Ponce were paid for. They would be on their way to Guatemala by air in less than forty-eight hours. It was also from there that monies were transferred to Belgium for Robbie's use. Then it was back to New York.

In Los Angeles, Anthony was keeping up the front. He had to keep Allison from getting too nosy. When the job came down, his and Washington's sudden absence might create questions. He had to figure some way to get rid of Allison for a couple of weeks, so he wouldn't be around to make waves or ask questions that were best left unasked. Anthony would have to talk with his father about this.

Hooker had done his job. His crew was lined up.
Now as soon as Washington returned from Bokala
and Robinson gave the word that everything was
ready in Belgium, they would be ready to begin the
final phase.

NINETEEN

It was coming together. Washington was back from Bokala. Robinson had his team on-line, as did Hooker. Through the Dutchman, Robinson had found a Canadian flight crew for the C-130. The crew had the kind of experience he needed. The C-130 was already in L.A.

Hendricks had personally supervised the shipment of Milt's Magic arsenal from Puerto Barrios to Grand Turk Island. Colonel Lima stood by until the cargo was loaded and in the air. The shipment was met on the other end by Tono.

Washington had stopped in D.C. on his way back and met with the Bokala consul, with whom he arranged for the stateside detachment to get their visas. Explaining that the technical crew was already stateside and that actors hired to play mercenaries were still in Belgium, Washington had arranged for Robinson's crew to obtain their Bokala visas in Brussels. There, they were stamped without question, as the consul in the United States had called his counterpart in Brussels, apprising him of the situation and instructing him to call President Okediji if he had any questions.

It was time for Hendricks to return to the States. Milton had left a week earlier. There was nothing to do now but bring it all together. He returned to the States via Mexico, taking a flight, as before, from Tapachula to Mexico City, but this time on to Tijuana rather than Miami. He crossed the border there with nothing but an athletic bag. He responded to the question of whether he was an American with a "yes" and to the question of whether he had anything to declare with a "no."

Once in San Diego, Hendricks met with Hooker, and together they drove to L.A. During the ride, Hooker informed Hendricks that Robinson's European crew had arrived earlier that day from Belgium.

They checked into one of the mid-class motels on the San Diego Freeway. Hendricks called Washington and young Anthony Collier from the motel. A meeting was set for the following day. He wanted everyone, including Hooker's and Robinson's men, to be present. Anthony and Washington, he wanted to see that night. For the meeting the next day, Hooker had arranged the use of a rehearsal hall in West L.A. No one would question a large group coming together in a rehearsal hall that was often used by film companies and dance groups.

Washington and Anthony came to Hendricks's motel room at eight that night. There, they went over the last details.

"Boss, I saw some of the men," Washington said the moment the motel door was closed.

"Who?" Hendricks asked solemnly.

"Sorry, Boss, not Duke or Claude, or young Calvin, but a handful of the others," Washington said. "They didn't look good, but they did look like they would survive for a while longer. Okediji made me wait a few days before I could see them. I imagine that was so he could clean them up and see to their physical condition first. When I did see them, it was without incident. I went in wearing huge sunglasses and a purple jump suit with a matching pith helmet. No one recognized me, or at least, they didn't seem to. Their treatment has been so severe that perhaps they no longer accepted what they saw as tangible."

"Were they the only ones left?" Hendricks asked.

"No, I don't think so. Kelo said there were more, and I believe him."

"Good," Hendricks said. "Now, how do we stand in Bokala?"

"Boss, it looks like it's all coming down. As far as Okediji is concerned, we have an open ticket. He wants this movie bad. I told him before leaving that I could not tolerate anyone messing with my equipment. I didn't mind having anything checked or opened, but I did not want ignorant people damaging anything. He said that he would see that there would be no problems with our gear. He would have Kelo there to supervise and clear things with customs."

"Very good, Washington. It seems you have carried off your end with a certain degree of finesse. Now, what about the men when they come in? Do you think Okediji will become suspicious when the team arrives in a C-130?"

Washington shook his head in the negative. "No, sir. I've already explained that we would be using the aircraft to recreate the battle scene at the airport. He was thrilled with the idea. The C-130 has already been loaded with enough cameras, lighting, sound and cable equipment to make the movie diversion believable. At Anthony's father's suggestion, I will be arriving this time by corporate jet. Robinson and Hooker will go with me as pilot and copilot of the company plane."

"Very good, Washington." Hendricks said. "You did good. I'm proud of you."

Washington swelled a bit. The boss didn't hand out compliments casually. When he said it, he meant it.

"Okay, Anthony. What's happening on your end? What are you going to do with Allison Chalmers?" Hendricks asked, turning his attention from Washington.

"It's already been done the easiest way possible. He's gone on vacation," Anthony said, smiling.

"Vacation?"

"Yes, sir. My father has invited him to come to our home in Bermuda, so they can discuss a bit of business and get to know each other better."

Hendricks smiled widely. "It really is coming together. I would like your father to keep Allison there for at least two weeks. Will that be a problem?"

Anthony laughed. "No. Allison was frothing at the mouth to spend time with my dad. The moment Dad told him to come, the poor son of a bitch nearly jumped out of his pants to get there. He knows where the money and power is; he'll stay as long as he is welcome. You can bet on that."

"It sounds like a sure thing all right," Hendricks replied. "Now, Anthony, you'll be traveling with me, Milton and the recruits. We'll depart for Grand Turk Island in the C-130 right after the meeting tomorrow. All the necessary passports and visas have been arranged for the group, right, guys?"

Hooker and Washington replied in unison. "Yes, Boss."

"Good. We won't have to clear customs or immigration on Grand Turk, but I want everything to be in order for Bokala. I don't want anything to tip our hand. The group in the C-130 will take on the weapons in Grand Turk, then go directly to Bokala. The recruits will learn Milt's Magic on the way from Grand Turk to Bokala."

Hendricks directed his next words at Washington. "Let's see the photos."

Washington handed Hendricks a large manila envelope filled with eight-by-tens of the airfield, bridges, the palace and the prison. Hendricks stopped at the second picture, his eyes going over the facade of the building where his men were being held.

"You know Kelo is one strange dude," Washington said. "I don't know how to read him. He's a hammer, though. Don't take no shit from no one. Anyway, he has this idea he'd like me to pass on to you, Boss. It's a plan on how to get our guys out."

"Go ahead, Washington. Spill it. We'll assume he's with us on this."

Washington smiled broadly. "It really is doable. I'm filming the airport scene using Bokala's elite squad; they all happen to be Okediji's tribesmen and members of the palace guard. Okediji is thrilled at having his tribesmen be the featured stars, and he is included in the scene, of course. He has already ordered Kelo to have a squad of replacements ready to take the duties of the palace guard when filming starts. The replacements will all be Kelo's tribes-men. We need only a handful of our men to rescue the prisoners. Kelo's men will do the rest. They will take care of any ministers, officials or clerks left at the palace. We will take our men directly to waiting vehicles and the airfield."

When Washington had finished, everyone in the group had a smile on his face.

"That's excellent. Our friend, Mr. Kelo, is a very smart man," Hendricks said. "We can be fairly certain now of what his game is. He's using us and we're using him. Fair's fair. But, I want everyone to keep an eye on him. I like him, but he's dangerous and, I believe, completely immoral in some aspects.

"Now, to incorporate Kelo's plan in with the strategy Hooker and I have been working on. Pay attention—a small detail forgotten could cost us all our lives. We have to get it all down now. Since Milton and Robinson are sitting on the recruits, they'll have to hear about it at the meeting tomorrow. The scheduled meeting time is 0600, so let's get down to it."

TWENTY

Washington leaned back into the soft leather of the Gulfstream's seat. He did not notice the opulent wood interior or rich country-club appointments of the cabin as Robinson piloted the plane high above the African landscape. He was lost in his own thoughts.

"Thirty seconds to show time," Robinson announced on the intercom.

Washington checked the time on the gold-and-diamond–encrusted Rolex strapped to his wrist as the now-familiar tarmac appeared. Dark patches covered the craters formed by mortars during Hendricks's last visit.

"Looks like they've rolled out the red carpet for you," Robinson's voice said over the speaker.

Looking closely, Washington could see the military formation set up on the runway. The sun reflected off the brass of a military band.

Rising from his seat, Washington made his way over the plush carpeting to the cockpit. He could see a thin smile spread over Robinson's lips as the luxury plane settled into a landing pattern.

Now the band, honor guard and trucks were in clear view on the runway.

"How does it feel to be a celebrity?" Robinson asked. The smile grew more amused.

"Nervous," Washington replied flatly.

"You'll get used to it," Robinson chuckled. "What do you say we give them real Hollywood entrance?"

"What?" asked Washington.

But Robinson wasn't talking to Washington. He was talking to Hooker, who was busily snapping switches on the overhead console.

"Sit down. Enjoy the show," Hooker said.

The tarmac was coming up quickly now. Washington could almost make out the faces of the men lined up on the edge of the runway.

Robinson began their approach, bringing the plane down, then at the last minute he pulled up slightly, buzzing less than a hundred feet over the heads of the assembled Bokala welcoming committee.

"Now that's the kind of entrance they'd expect a Hollywood mogul to make," Robinson said.

Washington sat silent as the plane banked at the end of the runway, turning to make another approach.

Washington inhaled deeply. He mentally braced himself for the days ahead. His last visit had been a social call. This time it would be something entirely different.

As Washington stepped down the G-6's short stairway, the Bokala army band broke into a halfhearted rendition of the country's national anthem.

Okediji strode toward him, arms extended and a wide smile breaking his face.

"Welcome, welcome back to Bokala, my dear Mr. Jones," he said, embracing Washington.

Then the sound of the C-130 broke from the

horizon. As the big plane lumbered toward them, Okediji's smile widened.

"We will need help unloading the equipment," Washington said. "Hollywood magic requires a great deal of equipment."

"Certainly, anything. Men will be put at your disposal, as many as you need."

At their first meeting, Okediji had seemed reserved, businesslike. But now, Washington noticed, he was as nervous as a virgin on prom night.

As the C-130 touched down, Okediji could barely contain his enthusiasm. He watched transfixed as the plane settled to a halt at the far end of the small runway.

Okediji raised his hand, and Kelo immediately appeared at his side.

"Go, welcome the rest of our guests. Make them comfortable, then help them unload," he said, not taking his eyes off the plane.

Instantly Kelo marched back into the ranks of Okediji's Leopard contingent, picking men for the honor of welcoming the Hollywood movie crew.

Washington breathed a sigh of relief. Among the mercs loaded in the C-130 was Hendricks, a man Washington was sure Okediji would not forget soon.

"We have much to discuss, much to do," said Okediji, wrapping a friendly arm around Washington and leading him off the runway.

The mercs moved quickly and professionally as they unloaded the C-130. Each bale of cable, steel container and light stand held an endless fascination for the Leopard soldiers, who helped the mercs transfer the equipment into trucks.

Hendricks watched from the side. He wore a pair of faded jeans and a black T-shirt advertising Jack Daniels. He drew no more attention than any of the other crew members. Never had an invading army come dressed so casually. Even their manner seemed carefree.

"Watch that case, guys, easy now," Milton said as the Leopards unloaded the equipment. The equipment seemed endless, but with Okediji's men doing most of the work, it went quickly for the mercs.

"Welcome to Bokala, gentlemen," said Kelo.

"Nice little country you got here," Hendricks replied, removing his drugstore sunglasses to look Kelo in the eyes.

"Yes, it is. Isn't it?" Kelo said, smiling.

"Bit hot, hotter than California."

"Yes, and no doubt it will get hotter," Kelo chuckled.

Milton had abandoned the task of overseeing the unloading to flank Kelo.

"And you must be?" Kelo said, turning toward Milton.

"Smith. The name's Smith," Milton said, his voice modulated into a neutral tone.

"Well, Mr. Smith, welcome to Bokala. You have your work cut out for you," Kelo replied, his good nature swelling up in a broad smile.

"We'll make do; we're professionals," Milton said.

"I certainly hope so. There is a great deal at stake," Kelo said. Then he turned abruptly away to give an order to one of his men.

"So that's Kelo," Milton said when Kelo was out of hearing.

"That's him," Hendricks replied.

"Goddamned cheerful, ain't he?"

"You'd be, too. He has the perfect setup. We win, he most likely gets a government," said Hendricks.

"We get our shit blown away, and he hasn't risked a fuckin' thing," Hooker finished.

"You got it."

Okediji's men stored the equipment in an empty hangar. Ancient deuce-and-a-half trucks transported Hendricks and the rest of the crew to Bokala's finest hotel.

"Now, just what would a movie crew do now?" Hendricks asked Hooker. He was lying flat on his back, staring at the cracked plaster and the broken ceiling fan.

"Get drunk. Come on to the local women. Stay in the hotel, seeing as Bokala isn't exactly known for its nightlife," Hooker said.

Hendricks rose slowly from the worn mattress. "That sound like a plan to you, Anthony?"

Hendricks had been worried about the boy. Since leaving Grand Turk Island the night before, he had shown no signs of nervousness, no emotion. A white-hot hate seemed to burn behind his eyes.

"Don't feel much like drinking," he replied from the rickety chair across the room.

"Okay, stay here. You'll get your chance soon enough."

And with that Hendricks and Hooker left the room.

"That kid's wrapped a little tight," Hooker said, as they walked down the hall.

"He'll be okay, I think he'll come through," Hendricks replied.

"He better."

By the time Hendricks and Hooker reached the hotel bar, most of the crew were already there. Hendricks was relieved to see that although they were loud, each closely watched the amount of liquor he consumed.

"Your men are having quite a good time their first night in Bokala, Mr. Jones," Okediji said.

"Yes, I imagine they are," Washington replied.

They were sitting in the dining room of the National Palace. Dinner was over, and Okediji was in an expansive and friendly mood. Sitting across the wide table, he leaned toward Washington as if to impart a secret.

"This movie will tell the truth," he said. "I have read the script you sent me. And it is the truth. But do you think American and European audiences will like it?"

"We did not come here to make a movie," Washington said, leaning toward the dictator.

Okediji's face went blank. His brow furrowed and his eyes suddenly opened wide. "No?"

"No, Mr. President, we did not," Washington said.

Suddenly a look of panic spread across Okediji's face. Had Hollywood somehow tricked him?

"Sylvester Stallone. You have heard of him? Rambo?" Washington asked.

"Of course," Okediji answered his countenance still twisted in puzzlement.

"Stallone, he makes movies," Washington explained. "Mr. President, we came here to make history. What we do here will make history in

America, Bokala and the world. They will know you by our work here."

Okediji's face relaxed. Yes, he knew now, the movie would be made. This Hollywood nigger would make the movie. And soon the whole world would know of Okediji and Bokala.

"Yes, of course, you are a man who takes his work seriously, I see," Okediji said, smiling.

Washington could feel himself relax. He was now in complete control. The nerves he had felt when he first entered Bokala were gone. He had a job to do, and he would do it.

"You molded a country, a people, by force of will," Washington said. "That is the way I will make my film. How could a union of two visions, two wills, not attract the attention of the world?"

"To our visions," Okediji said, lifting a half-filled wine glass.

"To Bokala," Washington replied, reaching out to tap Okediji's glass with his own.

TWENTY-ONE

The next day at sunrise, Hendricks and the rest of the crew were assembled in the hangar. The fifty men lounged about, sprawled on metal containers, spools of cables and other cinematic equipment. They pretended to nurse hangovers and complained of the early hour.

They stood out in sharp contrast to the one hundred elite Leopard forces who stood at attention at the opposite side of the building. Okediji's tribesmen were dressed in spotless uniforms. Even at attention, they seemed amused by the ragged group of Americans sprawled in front of them.

Kelo walked among his men, inspecting uniforms. But all eyes turned when Washington entered the building.

He walked with an air of supreme self-confidence. As Hendricks watched him, he mused that perhaps Washington was beginning to enjoy his role as a Hollywood director.

"Good morning. Today we start work," he said, his voice echoing in the cavernous building.

Without looking toward Kelo and his men, Washington walked directly over to Hooker, Milton and Hendricks. "The son of a bitch bought it, every damn inch," he whispered to Hendricks.

"Good. Now let's get this show on the road," Milton replied. "Let's show them some movie magic."

Milton walked slowly around the steel cases until he found the one he was looking for. He unsnapped the clasps and pulled from the foam cushions an FAL rifle, which he handed to Washington along with a full clip.

Washington strode out from among the men and approached Kelo.

"I will need a man for this demonstration," Washington said.

Kelo quickly pointed to a Leopard in the first column.

"This is an FAL assault rifle. Just like the ones used by the mercs," Washington said.

Kelo quickly translated into Bokalanese.

"You, step over there," Washington ordered to the "volunteer."

The man stood facing Washington, ten feet separating the two.

"This is one of the rifles we will use in the movie," Washington continued. "And this is how it works."

Before Kelo finished his translation, Washington had raised the weapon to his shoulder. The hangar exploded in an deafening echo of gunfire, as Washington let off a ten-round burst aimed at the volunteer's chest.

The volunteer let out a scream, reflexively raising his hands to stop the gunfire.

But no bullets ripped through his crisp uniform. Even before the echo of gunfire had died, the man knew that he was still alive, that he had been tricked.

The movie crew as well as the Leopard guards strained to suppress their laughter.

"Thank you," Washington said, indicating that the volunteer should get back into formation.

Kelo helped the man, still shaky, retake his place.

"It is only a toy. It is, like everything we do, make believe," Washington continued, as Kelo translated.

Now even Kelo could not help himself from grinning. This man, this director, had been well taught by Hendricks. And all at once the merc's plan became clear to the soldier.

An imposing ghetto blaster played the latest rock hit, filling the hotel bar with hot American guitar licks and a booming bass. A dozen beer-soaked cassettes lay next to the boom box. The music, which masked the mercs' conversation, was hardly needed. In just a few days the rowdy crew had become valued guests, both for the money they spent and their antics. Children pressed their noses against the smoked glass of the bar's windows, while the bartender smiled continually at the rich Americans' generous tips. He had made more in just two days than he would normally make in a year.

"Is it set for tomorrow?" Hooker asked, turning a smiling face toward the music.

"It's set," replied Hendricks. "Make sure that Washington arranges a little demonstration for Okediji. Nothing fancy, just enough to get the point across."

"Primacord and gas. We'll call it a rehearsal," said Hooker.

"And the lights. Spread the equipment out. That should take a full day, including mining the road," explained Hendricks.

"Right. After that stunt today with the rifles, none of Okediji's men believe anything we do is dangerous."

"Okay, just make sure that every one of Okediji's boys knows that the day after tomorrow is show time."

Suddenly, the music stopped, and the bar fell ominously silent.

"Goddamn that heavy metal bullshit," roared Robinson, getting up from the table and approaching the bar. Hendricks and Hooker watched him approach from the rear of the room. "Didn't any of you children remember to pack some honest-to-god American music?"

"Sit down, Pops," yelled one of the younger mercs. "Why waltz when you can rock 'n' roll?"

"No Johnny Cash? No Delbert McClinton? And no goddammned Hank Williams?"

Robinson strode up to the bar, grabbed the tape out of the box, threw it into the wall, grabbed another beer and threw a fistful of bills at the bartender.

One of the young mercs jumped up and slapped a new tape into the machine. "Forget you, old man," he cursed.

Robinson walked back to join Hendricks and Hooker at their corner table. "To success," said Hooker, raising the bottle.

"To show biz," said Milton, leaning in from the next table.

"To blowing Okediji's asshole out of that god-

damned palace and bringing our boys out," added
Robinson.

"And just what is this demonstration you have arranged," said Okediji, smiling. All morning the mercs
had been busy arranging the large C-lights, running
cable across the airport's tarmac and digging along the
roads. Soon, the world would know of Okediji.

"I thought this would amuse you," said Washington, signaling one of the film crew from across the
tarmac.

"Amuse me? Yes, practically everything you and
your men do amuses me."

Stefan Marcyzk stood at attention before the two
men. The Czeck soldier looked strangely out of
character wearing worn jeans and a grimy T-shirt.

"A film crew is like an army," said Washington.
"This man got drunk last night and was an hour late
for work. Is that a severe infraction in your army?"

But before Okediji could answer, Washington
pulled a 9mm pistol from his pocket.

"This is how we deal with drunkards," said Washington, rapidly firing three rounds into the Czeck's
midsection.

Marcyzk's shirt exploded with each round. The
big man staggered back, grasping his stomach and
crying out in pain as blood seeped between his
fingers.

Okediji's eyes glazed over at the sight. They
burned bright with the blood lust; he stood transfixed by the man who lay bleeding and groaning on
the dirt before him.

"Now, do you promise never to drink again,
Roth?" Washington smiled.

Instantly the Czeck jumped to his feet, smiling and nodding. Okediji stood there, stunned.

"Hollywood magic, my friend." Washington laughed. "Show him how it's done, Roth."

The Czeck stepped forward and ripped the bullet-ridden shirt from his body to reveal the exploded plastic bags of stage blood and the protective vest beneath.

"And the controls," Washington said, putting the weapon back into the pocket of his designer safari jacket.

Another merc stepped forward with a small transmitter.

"Truly amusing," said Okediji. "Ingenious, really." He laughed.

"And tomorrow, we start filming preliminary shots," said Washington. "But I will need to rehearse the elite Leopards."

"How many?"

"All one hundred of them, in full battle dress."

"Anything. Kelo will arrange everything for you. My best men, my tribesmen. Stardom will be their reward for defeating the dogs who invaded Bokala."

"Good. Excellent."

"And when will you need me? When am I to play my role?"

"Why, tomorrow at dawn. Tomorrow, you will be a star."

"Very good. Until tomorrow then," said Okediji as he turned and strode toward the palace doors.

Meeting again in the hotel bar, Hendricks, Robinson, Milton and Hooker went over the last details.

"Okay, Boss, the mines are laid around the airport," Hooker said.

"Good, what kind of mix did you use?" replied Hendricks.

"Primacord, high octane and C-4 in the runway service area. Alongside the road there's more of the same, with a mix of soap flakes and wire. Antipersonnel every hundred yards or so."

"No problems from Okediji's men?"

"Problems? They helped us. And goddamned if they're not out there now guarding the mines."

Hendricks couldn't help but smile. Mining the airport that afternoon, Okediji's men had been perfect helpers.

"And the Gulfstream?" asked Hendricks.

"It's fueled and waiting," said Robinson.

"Good. We'll take Okediji out on it. That will divert the Leopards away from our men in the C-130."

Milton ran one hundred of Bokala's finest through a crash course in acting that night. The lessons included running, firing the dummy weapons and dying.

"Remember I don't want to see any one of you getting up after you're dead," instructed Milton.

Kelo, who was translating, smiled at the instruction, as did most of the Leopards.

"These will be your weapons," continued Milton, his voice booming against the sides of the hangar. "Remember, fire as if the bullets are real—aim and fire."

The men nodded solemnly at Kelo's translation.

"Remember, the bullets cannot harm you." And to demonstrate his point, Milton pulled off a quick, three-round burst from the Uzi, then bent down and carefully picked up the shell casings.

Hendricks, in dark glasses, watched from atop a stack of packing cases. For an instant, his eyes locked on Kelo's. For a brief moment, Kelo smiled. For he knew that although Hendricks remained anonymous, he was the one behind the plan. Washington, Milton and the rest of them, took their orders from him. And it was Hendricks who would raise him to his rightful place as ruler of Bokala.

Hendricks nodded slightly, as if to affirm this secret information that passed between the two.

"That over there is the camera," continued Milton, pointing to the Aeriflex on mount. "Never, ever, look at it. Never acknowledge it."

And Kelo continued to translate.

As the African sun descended across the far end of the runway, the large Century lights bathed the airfield in an even, white glow. Bokala residents lined up three-deep along the chain-link fence that bordered the airfield.

At the palace, the twilit courtyard was about to be converted to day. The Barber of Bokala peered out the window into the courtyard; he could not contain his pride. Soon the world would know his name. Soon his deeds would be history. And he would be a legend.

So engrossed in his thoughts of cinematic glory was he that Okediji did not hear Kelo enter his study.

"Mr. Jones is ready for you at the airport," Kelo said.

Okediji turned to face his loyal soldier.

"Yes, I am prepared," he replied, fighting to keep the excitement from his voice.

"In hours, Your Excellency, they will start filming."

"That long?"

"They tell me it is exacting work."

"It is important work," Okejidi proclaimed. Turning to face Kelo, he laid his hand on the leather-bound script Mr. Jones had presented to him.

"Yes, it is important work," said Kelo and left the room.

The mercs worked in shifts. They were always visible to the ever-present crowd that lined the fence surrounding the airport. To the African onlookers, they merely seemed to be making last-minute adjustments on the large lights and running cable back and forth from hangar to runway.

Inside the hangar, Hendricks and the rest of the mercs re-armed their weapons. As promised, the small devices slipped out in seconds. Magazines of blank rounds were carefully packed away and replaced with live ammo that had been secreted at the bottoms of the dozens of steel cases.

The operation took a little more than an hour. And when they were through, Bokala still lay shrouded in night, except for the artificial glare of the Hollywood lights.

Hendricks sat on a case, checking the action of an FAL. Instinctively he felt the urge to fire the weapon, to make certain it still functioned with live rounds. But there was no time for that.

"It's show time," Hooker called from behind Hendricks. "Okediji's at the front gate."

Hendricks glanced down at his watch. Hooker was right; it was time for payback. From deep inside Hendricks could feel the hate rising. But hate was not what was called for now. There would be plenty of time for that later.

"Boss, it's time," Hooker called again.

"Right," Hendricks snapped. "Let's do it."

As Hendricks strode toward the two ancient deuce-and-a-half trucks, a pair of young mercs fell in behind him.

But even as they cleared the back gate of the airfield, Hendricks had to fight to keep it under control. He would have payment in full, Hendricks thought to himself as he forced a smile and a wave to the two Leopard guards stationed at the gate.

TWENTY-TWO

Hendricks was trembling when the door to the chambers below opened. He remembered clearly his feelings when Kelo had come for him. Now, he was back, and they were all going to get out. He knew the odds were better than even that not all would make it, but any odds were better than none. Kelo went in first; behind him were two young mercs carrying duffel bags. Hendricks entered last. Kelo tossed the ring of keys to the tallest of the three Leopards standing guard.

"Open them up and stand back," Kelo ordered.

The man saluted and moved down the stairs to the first cell and began unlocking it. The door opened. Hendricks moved past Kelo to look inside. A voice that tried to roar, but was too dry to do more than choke out the words, called to him from the dark interior.

"Ahh, Chef. There were times when I thought you were going to be late."

Becaude stumbled out into the corridor; Duke was behind him. Their faces were gaunt, washed out from the months without sun. They had aged fifteen years. Under the scraps of clothing they wore, their flesh hung loose on their bones.

Hendricks wanted to cry, but there was no time.

He spoke to Kelo, who nodded and took a duffel bag from one of the young mercs. Two Uzi smgs were passed over to Duke and Becaude.

Five of the fifteen years they had aged in prison immediately dropped off them.

From the other cells, the surviving mercs were pulled, carried and dragged into the hallway. Those who had the strength to walk helped the others. All of them asked for weapons, which were supplied from Pandora's olive-drab canvas bags. If they had to go down again, they wouldn't do it easily. There would be no more surrenders. Of that each had no doubt. They'd had a taste of the prisoner's life in the dungeons of the Bokala palace. They would not do it again.

A large figure carrying a smaller, emaciated figure under its arm brushed past Hendricks. He was glad to see the twisted, beaten-up face of Old Rudy the German. It would be a shame if no one ever heard him sing again. The old Wermacht veteran had one of the gentlest and purest voices Hendricks had ever heard.

Hendricks stopped Rudy for a second to see who he was carrying. It was Calvin, the young Vietnam veteran who'd been with the 173rd Airborne Brigade. The boy was alive, barely, and Hendricks wanted to keep him that way.

"Good, Rudy. Get on up to the top. We're going out and everyone is coming with us."

Rudy shifted his load and tried to speak. But all that came out of his mouth was a hoarse, rasping rush of air. Leaning his head to the side, Hendricks saw the reason. The Barber had played with Rudy.

His vocal cords were severed. The old German would not sing his songs around the campfire anymore.

As the prisoners came out of the cells, Hendricks did a count. It came up short. Men had died since he left, and of the twenty-three survivors, only seventeen were in fighting condition.

As they came out they were rapidly hustled up the stairs and over to the waiting trucks. Kelo's tribesmen helped. They didn't think much good about the white men, but with these, they felt they had something in common. All had suffered under the hands of the Barber of Bokala.

Duke and Becaude stayed with Hendricks. After this long, they didn't want to be separated again. From the barracks area, they heard firing and some screams, then silence.

"What's going on down there?" Becaude asked Hendricks and indicated the direction of the guards' barracks.

"They're getting rid of your jailers," Hendricks said. "All of them. These men"—he indicated the ersatz Leopards—"are from Kelo's people. It seems that the same thing is going down as when we came in. It's another coup. This time it's Kelo who's trying to take over."

Hendricks checked the time. They had to move fast. With communications to the city out, it wouldn't be long before someone got word to the army. They had to move before too many people realized something was up. It would take them half an hour to get back to the airfield.

"Okay," he said, "everyone outside to the trucks and get on board. Duke, Becaude, we don't have much time. If you want a chance to see Okediji paid off, we have to hurry."

Once outside the prison, where reception was better, Hendricks raised Anthony over the radio. "We got our people and we're heading out. How's it going there?"

"So far so good. Okediji is a little impatient for the filming to start. He has his men all placed and ready."

"Roger that. Have Washington do another run-through or something with the Leopards. It will keep them busy and show them where they are supposed to be when the shit goes down."

Kelo gave orders to a couple of his men, who rushed back into the prison.

"What are they doing?" Hendricks asked.

"I am going to release all the prisoners in thirty minutes. By that time you should be at the airfield, and it won't make any difference. But they can help me spread confusion in the city. I'm going to arm them with the weapons we've captured. There aren't enough for all of them, but when they come out, many will be ready for vengeance. If nothing else it may tie up some of Okediji's troops and police for a time."

Hendricks didn't care, but if that was what Kelo wanted, it was all right with him. He had what he had come for: his men. Anything else was superfluous.

"But remember, Kelo, we have to get back fast. If we don't take Okediji out, your takeover is going to be a lot harder."

Kelo grinned at him. "I know that. So why are we waiting here? Let's go make a movie."

Hendricks pulled a couple of bags from the rear of the second truck. Inside the bags were uniforms. He knew that just changing out of the prison rags would give his men's morale a large lift, and they would need it.

Once they were back in uniform and had weapons, they would again become a fighting force. In the past months, they had lost strength, but he felt that the hate they had inside them would compensate for that. It wouldn't be very long. If they were not out of Bokala—he checked his watch again—in two hours, it was not likely that any of them would ever be leaving.

"I'm going to ride in the rear truck with Duke and Becaude," Hendricks said to Kelo. "I can brief them on what's happening. Give me about ten minutes. Then when we pull off the road to back in through the rear gate of the airport, stop, and I'll move up to your truck with Becaude and brief the men there."

"All right, Hendricks. You got it. No problem, as you whites say."

Kelo left behind only five of his men, one to handle the telephone in case any calls came in and the rest to release the prisoners that filled the Bokala dungeon. As the trucks pulled out of sight, heading back to the airfield, the first of the native prisoners stumbled out into the courtyard, his body starved and gaunt, his hair matted and filled with insects and dried scum. The rims of his eyes were yellowish and filled with fever.

Two of Kelo's tribesmen guarded the outer compound. If any of the prisoners made a move to get out before the time limit, they would be killed. If they waited, then they would be given what weapons

there were in the armory of the prison. There were
enough to outfit eighty or ninety men with AK-47s
and some bolt-action model 98 Mausers.

The first prisoner to be released had been an
officer under Mehendi. He had killed before, and he
wanted to kill again—payback for the pain and
humiliation. He knew he was dying. Tuberculosis
was eating away at his lungs. He coughed a cracking,
chest-shaking, dry cough. He hacked up chunks of
lung tissue and gray fluid speckled with bright spots
of blood.

It was with great pleasure that Hendricks's men
threw off their prison rags and changed into uniforms. The new uniforms were of the same pattern
as the ones they had used when they first came to
this land of treachery built on treachery. They didn't
have full battle kits, but they had uniforms and
weapons. It would do.

The rear of the truck was covered now by a flap.
Between the former prisoners and the flap were ten
of Kelo's men. The tribesmen felt uneasy as they
watched the starved, bone-thin, white wrecks reach
eagerly for the Uzis. They felt even more uneasy as
the mercs worked the actions, took loaded magazines and slapped them against their heels to see the
rounds, and loaded the weapons. In a matter of
moments, they had changed from demoralized, be-
wildered and frightened prisoners into something
else. The bone-thin wrecks could kill, wanted to
kill.

Hendricks felt a swelling inside his chest as he
watched the change coming over his men. They had
looked like starved dogs, but now they were dogs
with new teeth that could tear and bite.

It took a sharp bark for him to make them keep their voices down. "All right. At ease! We still have some work to do, so listen up!"

Old habits and discipline returned. Becaude and Duke were assigned their sections. The op order was given. There would be no rehearsals this time. When it went down, they were to think of one thing: getting out. They were to kill anyone who got in the way.

But it had to be done with discipline. It had to be controlled killing. They were professionals, and they would act as such or they would never leave this cursed land of tears and blood.

Hendricks looked closely at the faces around him. He separated the sick and near sick from those still able to fight effectively. The near sick would take care of the very sick and hustle them to the waiting aircraft. Those able to fight were to give cover.

"Duke, Becaude, this is it. We have only about twenty minutes till things start to go down." He filled them in about the film crew and the rehearsal, which would be staged in less than twenty minutes. There were grins that showed canine teeth as the plan was explained. Several had to thump comrades on the back to keep laughter from breaking out.

There was a swerve, and the texture of the road under the tires changed. The hum of blacktop was gone. Now, there were the bumps and swaying that told them they were off the main road and on the track that led to the rear gate of the airfield. The trucks shuddered to a stop.

Hendricks jumped out and Duke was behind him. The mercs in the front truck would be under Duke's command. Hendricks moved past the men in the rear of the front truck to where he could speak to Kelo through the canvas flap separating the cab from the rear.

Duke silenced the men and began his briefing, filling them in on all that Hendricks had told him. They had their orders, and there was no other way out. The expressions on the faces of the men varied. Several had a faintly amused smile, others a sullen, serious, weary look. Fear of death was not there. They had gone too far for that. If there was fear, it was fear that they might have to go back to the cells of Bokala Prison. Before they would allow that to happen, they swore to themselves and each other that first they would die, and in the dying, take many with them.

Hendricks talked through the tarp to Kelo. "We have to get inside the gate without any problems, if possible."

Kelo nodded without taking his eyes off the dirt road ahead. "I know," he said. "But I will tell you this because I may not have the chance later. This is the last time I want to see you in my country. If you come here again for any reason, I will kill you. That is not a threat, it's a promise. Your kind here means no good. Therefore, once this is done, stay away. This is all I ask of you."

Hendricks almost smiled. It was always good to know the truth. "You got it, Kelo. I owe you that much. I will never come here again. But I want you to know that I will never forget you. You are one hell of a man in anyone's book. It has been good working with you. If you're ever in Guatemala, look me up. I'm not hard to find."

Kelo nodded. He did not turn his head to look at

Hendricks. "As you say, it has not been all bad. But now I think you should check in with your people at the field. We are almost at the gate."

"Right you are," Hendricks said. Then he clicked on the RT and spoke into the mouthpiece. "This is Hendricks. How copy, over?"

Static, then Anthony came back. "Roger. We read you five by five. What's your twenty?"

"We are coming up on the rear gate. Should be on site in one-zero minutes. Over."

"Roger. Ten is about all I think you got. It looks like the thing is going down at any moment. There's no way to stall any longer."

"Roger that. Do what you got to do. We'll be with you in ten. Out."

TWENTY-THREE

No one spoke on the ride to the airfield. Hendricks sat in the back of the truck with Duke and the rest. Rudy crouched at the end of the bench, working the bolt of an FAL rifle again and again, checking the clip with palsied hands that caressed the weapon with frightening, deadly intensity. Except for an occasional grinding of the truck's gears, the clicking of Rudy's FAL was the only sound as the truck raced along.

Once again Hendricks felt black hate rising up in him. Looking into the gaunt faces of his men, into their burning eyes filled with murderous vengeance, only fueled his own lust for payback.

Then it hit him. The whole absurdity of it came crashing down around him. He was leading a band of seventy men, lightly armed, against a well-armed African dictator. Of all the weapons in his pathetic arsenal, deception was the most lethal.

The truck did not slow down when they approached the gate. Kelo leaned out of the passenger door, one foot on the running board, signaling and yelling for the guards to open up.

Back in the safety of the hangar, Hendricks helped unload the wounded men.

"Are you all right?" Kelo asked Hendricks, after

they had made the wounded as comfortable as
possible.

Hendricks stood mute, watching old Rudy continue to caress his weapon. Okediji might have cut
the voice from his throat, but Rudy would have no
trouble making his feelings known.

"Afraid, perhaps?" Kelo said, a slightly mocking
quality coming into his voice. "Well, it's too late for
that now."

Hendricks turned toward Kelo. It took just one
look at the merc leader's face to melt Kelo's smile.

They stood like that for a moment, Kelo unable to
pull his eyes away from Hendricks. The young
African warrior had seen many things written across
men's faces in the heat of battle, under torture, even
when they were dying at the hands of a bitter enemy.
But he had never seen a look as frightening as the
one he saw in the white American's eyes.

Without another word, Kelo broke away from the
horrible stare and walked toward the back exit of the
hangar.

Soundlessly, Hendricks strode to the hangar's
door. At the gate of the airfield, a small group of
Bokala soldiers stood easy guard. They chatted with
the gawkers, posturing and smoking cigarettes.

Another guard stood near the hangar's door.

Hendricks motioned him over. Smiling, he leaned
his weapon against the corrugated steel of the building and walked into the dimly lit building.

As Hendricks engaged the guard in sign-language
conversation, Hooker approached from the rear, his
Gerber combat knife held down against his right
pant leg.

"You know, we have a saying back home," said

Hendricks to the uncomprehending guard. "If you can't do it on nicotine, alcohol or pussy, then don't do it."

The guard broke into a huge, uncomprehending grin. But the grin quickly changed to a look of panic as Hooker grabbed him over his nose and mouth and cut deep across his throat in one fluid motion.

A river of blood flowed through the gaping second mouth Hooker had opened. The guard's hands instinctively flew to the savage wound, his mouth silently trying to muscle a scream from the cut vocal cords.

He was dead in seconds.

"It's show time," Hendricks said as he walked toward the truck.

Hooker followed immediately, pausing only long enough to bend down and wipe the bloodied blade of his knife against the dead Bokalan's pant leg.

Okediji studied his reflection in the mirror. The Gulfstream's bathrooms were an embarrassment of marble and gold appointments. But Okediji felt at home in such luxury. Preening, he examined every inch of his spotless uniform. Soon the world would know his name. Far off he could hear the sound of gunfire. Instinctively, his muscles tensed beneath the crisp fabric of his uniform. His chest swelled under countless medals of his own design.

"It won't be long now," Washington said from outside the door.

The dictator remained silent, straining to hear the sounds of battle.

"We're doing some preliminary shots," Washington said.

"Why are you not out there directing, Mr. Jones?" Okediji said, stepping out of the chamber.

"Because that is not my job. My assistant director films the unimportant scenes. I will personally direct you and your Leopards," Washington replied.

Okediji visibly swelled again. "Makeup, I have not been made up," the dictator stammered.

"The makeup man should be here momentarily," Washington answered.

"Wait, one moment please. May I trouble you to help me study my lines?"

Washington couldn't believe it. Everything was going down, and now Okediji wanted to study his lines, like some damn Marlon Brando. Furiously, the dictator raced about the plane's cabin looking for the leather-bound volume.

"Here, here, I have found it," he said, raising the script up victoriously.

"Good. Then let's practice," Washington said with relief.

"Yes, yes, by all means."

"Relax, Your Excellency," Washington said as they went over his lines again and again. "You'll be the Clint Eastwood of Africa."

"Clint Eastwood, yes. But was not your own Ronald Reagan an actor?" Okediji enthused.

"Before he became president," Washington replied. "You'll be the first president-actor."

Okediji was so caught up with thoughts of Clint Eastwood and Ronald Reagan that he did not look through the plane's windows. If he had, he would have seen that something horribly wrong was going on at the far end of the runway.

"My dear Mr. Jones," Okediji said suddenly. "Why

are we sitting in this stifling aircraft? Should we not be on the, ah, set?"

"In Hollywood the stars always get a luxury trailer. This will have to do."

"Yes, yes, of course."

"Damn, the makeup man must be late," said Washington as they finished going over Okediji's lines for the twentieth time.

Then Okediji saw it. One of the film workers motioned a Leopard over. The Leopard walked casually toward the tall American. And just as casually the American pulled a pistol from his belt and shot him.

It was a clean shot to the head. The Leopard's skull exploded in a rain of bone, brain and blood against the white hangar door.

Okediji rose from the leather seat, panicked. But before he could take two steps on the richly carpeted aisle, Washington was on him, blocking his escape.

"That's it, motherfucker, sit the fuck down," Washington said.

"I do not understand," Okediji replied, walking toward Washington.

Instantly, a 9mm Baretta appeared in the merc's hand, drawn from one of the deep pockets of his safari jacket.

"You'll understand soon enough," Washington said, motioning him back to his seat.

But Okediji kept walking toward the merc.

"Sit the fuck down!" Washington screamed.

"But, Mr. Jones, we are sensible men. What is it you want?"

Washington pulled the trigger, sending a round

between Okediji's feet. The room was filled with the
sound of the blast.

The first Leopards were easy. They came running
out carelessly to meet their death. Those who fired
sent a barrage of blank rounds at the mercs, who
returned fire with the real thing.

The gunfire brought more Leopards running from
around the hangar and their posts at the airfield. For
a moment they froze, they smiled at the sight of
their comrades lying bleeding and dying on the
tarmac—more movie trickery.

Then they saw. They saw that the blood and the
dying were real. A moment of panic set in. The first
one to fire did so tentatively.

"Goddamn, here comes the real thing," the young
Czech said from behind the cover of a jeep.

In an instant, the airfield was blazing with the
sound of automatic weapons. Although outnum-
bered, the mercs had the advantage of surprise.
Leopards fell by the tens as Rudy sprayed the tarmac
with his FAL.

From behind him one of the mercs fired an RPG
into an oncoming column of Leopards. When the
smoke cleared, the charred remains of a dozen men
lay scattered where the round had found them.

Soon the airport belonged to the mercs. The floor of
the control tower was slick with blood. The four
controllers and their supervisor were laid out neatly
on the floor, their throats cut.

Then it came. The unmistakable sound of mortar
fire. The shit was hitting the fan.

Fortunately the guards at the front gate were still

smiling. In the confusion, nobody had taken the time to radio them.

"Neutralize the gate," Robinson barked at a young merc. There were not more than thirty Leopards ranging the airfield now. Four were at the main gate. A handful were defending the pride of the Bokala air force, an aging Mig that had not been airborne in years, because of lack of either parts or trained personnel.

Washington watched the fighting from the front cabin of the Gulfstream. The small window wouldn't provide much protection from a stray round.

Then the aircraft shuddered. A tremendous explosion brought it up off its wheels, knocking Washington back across a writing desk that protruded between a couch and the bar.

"Goddamn," he cursed, looking back at his prisoner.

"What, what is going on?" Okediji stammered.

Pulling himself up off the floor, Washington gazed through the small window at clearing smoke. Near the starboard wing, Okediji's limo sat in a pile of twisted metal and flames.

"Mortar," Washington said.

"The fools, the fools," Okediji replied. "do they not know I am in here?"

"They took out your ride," Washington said with dismay. "And part of the wing, which means my ride, too."

Robinson had seen the mortar hit the limousine. The limo's gas tank went instantly. Flames now licked at the Gulfstream's wings and fuel tank.

Robinson climbed into a battered jeep and headed

toward the Gulfstream, at the far end of the gate. The tarmac was littered with the bodies of dead Leopards. Several times he had to swerve the vehicle to avoid running over the remains of one of Okediji's finest.

He approached the aircraft with his horn blazing. They didn't have much time. Soon a second wave of Leopards would arrive, and they wouldn't be as easy to fool.

Before the jeep came to a full stop, Washington and Okediji appeared at the Gulfstream's door. The dictator had his hands bound behind his back. Washington followed with a smile, prodding him along with the barrel of the 9mm.

Robinson hurried them into the jeep and drove across the blazing tarmac. Before they had cleared fifty yards, the Gulfstream blew. The explosion of jet fuel and corporate luxury came at their backs in a great wave of intense heat.

"Goddamn, that was one nice ride," Washington moaned as he looked back at the fireball rising high into the air.

"One thing less for Kelo to nationalize," Robinson replied.

"Kelo? Kelo, is he the dog behind this?" Okediji put in.

"You better just shut up, or I'm gonna blow your shit away right here," Washington ordered the dictator, nudging the gun uncomfortably up under his nose.

After depositing Washington and Okediji at the hangar, Robinson drove off to the main gate. When the Leopards showed up, that's the way they would come.

The African sun was high now. Robinson, Claude and Duke would lay down ground fire at the gate if Hendricks, Hooker and the Czech needed it. Other mercs were posted at the hangar door, and on the roof.

Next to Robinson was the remote for the mines along the highway and perimeter of the airport. Climbing out of the jeep, he grabbed the remote and the FAL.

"Lock and load," he told the mercs.

They took their positions behind the truck. The sound of mortars was replaced by that of small-arms fire.

Then they heard them.

When trucks appeared at the first rise in the road, Robinson tapped off charges with a remote.

A fireball rose over the trees in the distance.

Robinson hit the remote again, and the first jeep vanished in a fiery wall of primacord napalm. Even from a distance, Robinson could see the broad smile of Becaude from behind the FAL as he watched the jeep veer off the asphalt and into a shallow ditch.

But the two other jeeps and an APC had gotten through.

Robinson heard fire from his snipers on the roof. Shots rang off the APC like angry bees. The lead jeep's window shattered, but it kept coming.

Robinson shouted for the two mercs to drop back. They climbed back in the truck after setting off the rest of the charges with the remote.

The sound was nearly deafening. In an instant the airstrip was engulfed in flames. The air smelled richly of gasoline.

Robinson and the mercs raced across the blazing

tarmac. Looking back, Robinson could see that the two jeeps and the APC had made it through the mines.

Then the lead jeep took a bullet in the front tire. Spinning wildly out of control, it flipped twice, leaving a trail of glass and bent olive-green metal. Wounded Leopards lay along the way.

The snipers had come off their perches now. They had taken cover in the doorway of the hangar. Shots rang off the armor of the APC, but the damn thing kept coming. Its .50 covered the entrance to the hangar with withering fire.

Across the airfield the C-130 started its engines. But even as its giant engines choked and whined to life, the APC closed the gap between the airport's buildings and the plane.

Glancing to his left, Robinson saw more Leopard troops streaming through the fence. They were coming in jeeps, in trucks and on foot.

"Son of a bitch," Hendricks cursed from the hangar. He crouched in the shadow of the hangar's door, squeezing off shots from an FAL. Old Rudy tapped shots from the opposite side of the door. Near Hendricks, the snipers were at work. But there were just too damn many Leopards.

The hangar was now the focus of the Leopards' fire. Behind him, Hendricks could hear their rounds ricocheting off the steel beams of the hangar. He knew it was only a matter of time before the corner they were trapped in got smaller and smaller.

"Get ready to move out," he called over his shoulder. The injured and dying men had been left in the trucks. Hendricks soon heard the sound of the truck engines starting to life.

The C-130 stood with its rear cargo doors open and waiting.

As one of the trucks passed into the open, Hendricks jumped on the running board, tapping off shots at the advancing APC.

The fire from its .50-caliber machine gun snapped at the tires of the two deuce-and-a-half trucks. Hendricks knew what he had to do. Jumping from the truck's side, he hit the ground running, his FAL laying down a careful cover against the APC.

Five young mercs followed him from the back of the other truck. Using the crashed jeep as cover, they would hold off the APC.

No sooner had they gained the cover of the jeep, than Hendricks heard the sound of mortar fire. A black, smoking hole in the tarmac opened up a hundred yards away from the C-130, but it wouldn't take long for them to find the range.

Directly in front of them, the overturned jeep was taking a beating from the .50 of the APC, which couldn't have been more than fifty yards away.

"We gotta get that son-of-a-bitch," Hendricks muttered.

"I'll get the gunner," said Anthony from beside him. "You toss out the grenade."

Hendricks hadn't realized that one of the young mercs who had followed him out on the tarmac was Anthony. Now he was glad of it. The young man had come through.

"Okay, sounds like a plan " Hendricks said, unsnapping a grenade.

Anthony snapped a fresh clip into his FAL and crawled to the mortar hole at the edge of the jeep's battered frame.

The APC was less than thirty yards from them now. It had slowed up, the driver wary of what lay behind the bullet-ridden wreckage.

"Now!" Hendricks hissed, grenade in hand.

The other mercs rose from their positions. With the first burst of their fire, the machine ceased.

Hendricks jumped up an instant later, in a smooth arc toward the now-stopped APC. There was a horrible second when the only sound was Anthony's and the other mercs' fire.

Then the grenade blew. It had caught the Leopards as they prepared to leave the APC and kill off Hendricks and his young comrades.

"Move it out!" cried Hendricks. "To the plane!"

TWENTY-FOUR

Okediji's warriors were rallying rapidly to him. The mercs at the machine shop were trying to break contact. They had made one sally to finish off the Leopards. They were to break contact and head for the planes.

They had started across the field when machine gun fire raked the strip. A machine gunner at the far end had awakened and begun laying fire. Two men went down with leg wounds. The femur of one was splintered; pieces of bone stuck out of his red-and-green camouflage trousers. He was dragged back to the machine shop by the others. It didn't take long. Only seconds had passed. Seconds were often the difference between success and failure, living and dying.

Hendricks and the five men with him ran across the field. From the mortar pit, Anthony lay down machine gun fire to counter the other gunner and keep him off Hendricks. Even with the interference of Anthony's suppressive fire, the other gunner managed to send several bursts skipping along the tarmac.

Hendricks felt a burning sensation inside his left thigh. It felt as if someone had struck a kitchen match on his leg.

They were on the field. It was déja vù as Hendricks raced past the guards manning the machine gun post at the entrance to the runway service area. Waving for them to follow, he moved straight for the C-130. The motors were running. Robinson, Becaude and Duke leaped out of the truck and raced onto the plane. Robinson would now pilot this plane instead of the Gulfstream as previously planned. But no one, by God, would be left behind this time.

Okediji was in a sullen rage, hands tied behind him with nylon cuffs, his uniform wrinkled and sweaty. They would pay for this. As soon as they landed, he would be turned over to some kind of formal authority. He was, after all, the head of an independent state.

He would be set free, and when he was, he would take vengeance. He would hunt them all down, including the traitor Kelo. Hendricks would pay the highest price of all. If it took years and millions to do it, it would be done.

Beneath them the airfield rapidly reduced in size as they gained altitude. The tailgate was still open. Using the intercom to the cockpit, Hendricks gave an order, and the C-130 banked to port, taking up a new heading, which would run it over the center of the city.

Okediji was trying to stare down Duke and Becaude. He failed. They watched him as a hungry dog watches a steak bone. They wanted his ass. Okediji began to feel even more uneasy. As he looked down the aisle of the plane where men sat strapped on canvas seats, all of the eyes were on him. Many of them had come from the cells of his prison. He knew that if their leader, the man called Boss or sometimes Chef, let them, they would tear him apart with their bare hands.

The temperature began to drop as they gained more altitude, reaching eight thousand feet as Okediji's capitol passed beneath him.

Hendricks saw Okediji watch the men in the plane. It was time. Time for payback. The scars on his chest tingled. Duke's, then Becaude's, gaze touched his. No words were spoken, but they knew without a doubt that a debt was soon to be settled. Not just for Hendricks—this payoff was for all of them.

They leaned forward in the seats. What they felt was somehow transmitted to the others in the plane. They watched Okediji with hollow, burning eyes, not knowing what was going to happen but not wishing to miss a second of it. They tried not to blink, afraid that what would take place would happen in that blinking of an eye.

A chill ran over Okediji. Goose bumps rose up on his dark skin, and it was not from the cold of the higher altitude. He felt the thing that had passed among the captives. Sweat gathered and ran down his spine in spite of the lower temperature.

Slowly, he turned his head to see Hendricks's eyes on him. Hendricks smiled a thin smile, lips drawn tight over his teeth. Okediji's eyes moved down. A movement of Hendricks's hand toward his balls caused adrenaline to run through Okediji's veins.

"No," he whispered, "you cannot do this. I am the leader of an independent state, president of the Republic of Bokala." Hendricks said nothing. His free hand moved a flick of the wrist to open the straight-edge razor of Soligen steel. It had never been used.

"I demand to be brought before an international court. If you think I have committed a crime, I have a right to a trial. You are not authorized to do anything. You must take me back. Or you will be a criminal in the eyes of the world!"

Hendricks moved closer to him, nodding to Duke and Becaude to come to him. Releasing their seat belts, they moved forward, each taking one of Okediji's arms, gripping him firmly as the winds outside were whipped up by the blast of the props. Cool, clean air rushed over them in waves.

Hendricks moved closer to Okediji, not wanting his words to be lost in the roar of prop blast.

"I am already a criminal in the eyes of the world. We are all criminals here. But you are something else—an animal gone mad. And you do know what is done, even in the civilized world, to mad dogs. Don't you?"

Okediji felt his throat constrict. He wanted to cry out. There was death, his death, in the white man's eyes. No! He was the leader of his people, he would not give this "mercenary" the satisfaction of seeing him weak. If death was to come, he would face it as he had before in his life. He was the leader of a race of warriors. Death he had faced before, and death he had given. He would die like a warrior. If they were going to kill him, it would be done in the Western fashion. A shot to the head. The razor in the mercenary's hand was no more than a threat to make him weak. Cold steel was not their way.

Hendricks undid the first three buttons of his shirt. The scars showed clearly on his flesh. "Remember, Okediji, when you did this? I was not the only one you shaved. Now it is your turn."

He held the razor up close to Okediji's face,
touching the dark, flushed skin with the cold, sterile
edge. The memory of those he had shaved in his life
rushed over the Barber. The fear he had promised not
to show came in a flood. A hot, wet flood that ran
down his trousers legs.

He was going to die.

"Before me, before my men, you have faced your
court, and you know the punishment." Nodding to
Duke and Becaude to tighten their grip, Hendricks
sliced the buttons off of Okediji's tunic one by one,
exposing the sweaty flesh beneath.

Next, with one hand, he undid Okediji's broad
leather belt and cut off the first two buttons of his
trousers.

Okediji wanted to scream. His mouth was too dry
to make words or cries. The best he could do was a
long, undulating whimper. Hendricks placed the
razor on Okediji's flesh just above the black, curly
pubic hair. This time the white man would cut.
Okediji knew that. With startling clarity, he knew
that and was terrified of what was to happen next.

The razor moved up. Hendricks applied pressure.
Firm, solid, and slow, the iced steel of the Soligen
razor slid with grace and ease through the flesh of
Okediji's body, up from the region of the pubis, going
deeper every inch. The good German steel split his
navel in two, and still Hendricks slid the razor
higher, slicing deeply through the thin skin of the
solar plexus until it reached the bony plate of the
sternum and slid out.

Okediji did not feel any great pain, but he knew
that would pass as the flesh behind the razor's
incision opened up. At first it would be just a thin,

red line held together by the glue of his own body fluids. Then it would open, open wider and wider—the longer the slice, the wider the opening.

He was right. He should have been. The razor had been his toy for years. The cut did open wider, from the pubis to the sternum, a quarter inch at first, then a full inch, then two. Okediji felt his intestines trying to bulge out through his flesh and escape from the confining pressure of his abdomen.

Stepping back, Hendricks grabbed Okediji by his shoulder and shoved the razor deep inside the Barber's body cavity, making a circle with his hand, slicing and cutting. Now Okediji found the strength to scream.

Hendricks let loose the razor. His hands found something else. He began to pull and jerk inside Okediji's stomach. His hand came free, holding a bulge of intestinal coils.

He nodded at Duke and Becaude. They released their grip on Okediji. The screams were coming as if from a thin wind through the branches of a desert tree. Okediji did not break for breath.

Hendricks pushed him to the edge of the ramp, where the city lay below. The pilot had gone into a tight orbit. Hendricks could feel the increasing pressure that tried to move him back against the side of the aircraft. He fought it, pushing Okediji to the edge of the ramp. Then, he whispered softly into Okediji's ear, not knowing or caring if he could be heard.

"Time to shave the Barber."

He pushed. Okediji fell into the prop blast, his mouth open, his screams drowned by the roar of the motors. Hendricks stood on the ramp and held on to a strap. His right hand still held the slippery, rubber-like roll of intestinal tissue as it trailed out behind the falling body of Okediji.

Then it was jerked from his hand. Okediji had reached the end of his line.

DANIEL STRYKER

HAWKEYE

"A grabber of a story!"—Mark Berent,
bestselling author of <u>Steel Tiger</u>

In this electrifying new novel of international crisis and response, the author paints a chilling and authentic scenario of the ultimate conspiracy. Superpower technology is under attack. The enemy is unknown. And Defense Intelligence agent Dalton Ford must follow a shocking trail of high-tech sabotage into the brutal heart of worldwide terrorism.

__0-515-10509-0/$4.50

COBRA

"Taut, exciting. A trip into a whole new
field of thriller fiction."—Tom Clancy

On the cutting edge of military technology, this electrifying thriller unveils the startling realities of tomorrow's wars. The weapons and planes are state-of-the-art. The enemy is a dangerous new coalition of international forces. And the U.S.-Soviet test-pilots and crew are prepared to launch a devastating new form of air combat. This time, it's not a test...

__0-515-10706-9/$4.50 (On sale Nov. 1991)

CASCA

THE ETERNAL MERCENARY
by Barry Sadler

___ #1: THE ETERNAL MERCENARY	0-515-09535-4/$3.95
___ #12: THE AFRICAN MERCENARY	0-515-09474-9/$2.95
___ #14: THE PHOENIX	0-515-09471-4/$3.50
___ #15: THE PIRATE	0-515-09599-4/$2.95
___ #16: DESERT MERCENARY	0-515-09556-7/$2.95
___ #20: SOLDIER OF GIDEON	0-515-09701-2/$3.50
___ #21: THE TRENCH SOLDIER	0-515-09931-7/$3.50
___ #22: CASCA: THE MONGOL	0-515-10240-7/$3.50